"Bitch!" a woman screamed.

Brett didn't think, she reacted. In just the flash she'd seen, she knew what the brunette had pulled, and she flew, taking the most direct route, leaping up and running across tabletops to the dance floor. Pushing aside several women who were just realizing what was happening, Brett grabbed the brunette's arm, her gun arm, and pushed it up. Brett shoved her other arm between the two women so that the drunk sailed backward onto the relative safety of the floor.

Titles by Therese Szymanski

Available from Bella Books

The Brett Higgins Motor City Thrillers

When the Dancing Stops
When the Dead Speak
When Some Body Disappears
When Evil Changes Face
When Good Girls Go Bad
When the Corpse Lies
When First We Practice

New Exploits

(with Karin Kallmaker, Julia Watts & Barbara Johnson)
Once Upon a Dyke: New Exploits of Fairy Tale Lesbians
Bell, Book and Dyke: New Exploits of Magical Lesbians

Edited by

Back to Basics: A Butch-Femme Anthology
Call of the Dark: Erotic Lesbian Tales of the Supernatural

When First We Practice

THERESE SZYMANSKI

2005

Bella Books, Inc.
P.O. Box 10543
Tallahassee, FL 32302

Printed in the United States of America on acid-free paper
First Edition

Editor: Anna Chinappi
Cover designer: Sandy Knowles

ISBN 1-59493-045-7

For Peyton and Ian

O, what a tangled web we weave,
When first we practise to deceive!
Sir Walter Scott (1771–1832)

About the Author

Reese ran away from her home state of Michigan at the tender age of thirty. She used to spend far too much time hanging about unsavory neighborhoods in Detroit. Now she resides in the nation's capital where she uses copywriting and designing to keep herself apartmented and stocked with Miller Lite and nicotine gum. An award-winning playwright, she's been a Lammy finalist in two categories—mystery and erotica—made the Publishing Triangle's list of notable lesbian books for 2004, been short-listed for a Spectrum Award, and had stories in a number of Lammy finalist books. She writes the Brett Higgins Motor City Thrillers, has edited a couple of anthologies, including the upcoming *The Perfect Valentine: Erotic Lesbian Valentine's Day Stories*, is part of the team that created *Bell, Book and Dyke: New Exploits of Magical Lesbians* and next year's *Stake through the Heart: New Exploits of Noir Lesbians*, and has contributed to more than a dozen anthologies.

She enjoys backpacking, weightlifting, all forms of skiing, and anything else she can hurt herself doing, including urban surfing and running with scissors. Somehow, through the years and sometimes without her consent, she's started collecting medieval weaponry, Zippos and bears. (Well, she also collects *Buffy the Vampire Slayer* action figures, but only because they're just so darned handy for blocking complex action sequences in her writing.)

You can e-mail Reese at tsszymanski@worldnet.att.net—preferably only when *not* trying to get her to buy a timeshare, join your religion, spend money on weird new sexual devices or pyramid schemes, or help you move money from Nigeria.

Prologue

September 13, 1996 11:21 p.m.

Rowan Abernathy and Allison Sullivan searched the quiet suburban street for the "lurking figure" someone had phoned in about to the Southfield Police Department. Rowan drove while Allie used her big Maglite to search the neighborhood.

"Stop," Allie said to Rowan, jumping out of the car. One hand was on her gun, the other still clutched the Maglite.

Rowan parked at the curb and ran up behind her.

"Stop and . . ." Allie said, pulling her gun and edging toward the teenaged boy who stood in the front bushes. She sighed and holstered her gun. "Can I help you with something?" She'd seen him lurking in the bushes, but really, he just looked like some scrawny punk kid up to some practical jokes shortly before Halloween. She didn't see any weapons, and he wasn't very large. Obviously some snoopy neighbor was sitting on the panic button.

"Uh, no," he looked around nervously, almost like he maybe *did* have something to hide.

This got Allie's attention. She dropped her hand to again lie casually on her gun. "What's going on here?"

"Nothing, I was just taking a walk," the boy said, pulling himself up to his full, rather impressive height.

"In the bushes at night. Yeah, right," Allie said.

"Keep an eye on him while I take a look around," Rowan said to Allie, while she slowly edged around the residence.

"Just stay put," Allie told the kid, and she glanced around. They needed to make sure he hadn't been vandalizing the house or breaking into it. Allie quickly assessed the location of the vehicles on the street, checking to see if anything was out of the ordinary. She thought she saw movement in one, about a half block away, and so she started toward it. It was quite late for anyone to be out and about in this neighborhood if they weren't up to mischief.

"Do you see something?" Rowan said, stepping from the far side of the house.

"That car, down the street?" Allie said.

"What . . . Watch out!" Rowan screamed, suddenly running at Allie and tackling her.

Allie didn't register what was going on before she heard the gunshot. The next thing she knew, Rowan was lying on top of her.

"Ow." Allie had her gun out by the time she'd rolled Rowan off her. She pulled up into a crouch, looking for their attacker as she kept her center of gravity low. What she saw was the previously assumed young vandal running into the house. "Are you all right?" she asked Rowan.

"I'm shot."

"How bad?" Allie knew if Rowan was able to talk, that was good.

"In the butt."

"We need to get you out of here," Allie said, pulling out her radio.

Chapter One

Wednesday, 2:23 p.m.

Detroit was no longer the easiest place in the world to be murdered. It was no longer filled with burnt-out streetlights, potholed roads, and burned down buildings. New construction was taking place in even the most questionable of neighborhoods, such as the Cass Corridor. The man who had reigned as mayor during much of the city's downfall was long gone, buried, and pretty much forgotten.

Detroit was no longer the hands-down winner for Murder Capital of America.

But it would still be as stupid to wander the streets in many neighborhoods after dark as it would be to play football on the slopes of Aspen on the last run of the day. Improvement to anything usually comes slowly, and cosmetic changes are easier than real ones. Those who don't pay attention to that simple fact might as well slam into a tree while doing seventy skiing the trees at Heavenly à la Sonny Bono.

Of course, none of this crap mattered much to Brett Higgins and Allie Sullivan who lived in Royal Oak, just a stone's throw north of Detroit along the Woodward corridor. Ferndale, just south of them, was rapidly getting the nickname of "Dykedale."

The Detroit area was home, regardless of the drug dealers, prostitutes, criminals, gangs, and anything else that an outsider might hold against the city. Besides, Brett Higgins was on a first-name basis with quite a lot of the so-called criminal element, having been an active part of that community for many years. Allie herself was an ex-cop, and her ex-girlfriend was a Detroit detective.

"How's this?" Brett asked when she and Frankie moved the couch two inches to the right—for the third time.

Allie stood between the front windows and gazed at the room. "Yeah, that'll do for now." Brett frowned at the "for now." How much difference could a few inches one way or the other really make, for Christ's sake?

"Oh, no no no no no!" Kurt cried from next to Allie, "It simply must be moved exactly two-and-a-half inches to the left!"

Brett growled at Frankie's flaming boyfriend. Kurt looked back at her, tossed off a quick three-snap and stood with his hands on his hips.

"Oh, come now," Kurt said. "We *all know* how much you two love showing off those big butch muscles of yours." This time it was Frankie's turn to stop and stare at Kurt.

"Save it for the bedroom, boys," Allie said.

"It doesn't really matter anyway, you know," Maddy said, peering out of the kitchen. "She'll want to change everything in a few weeks regardless." Her red hair was tousled so it looked like a fire stack on top of her head. Even though Madeline was a bit on the plump side and several inches shorter than Brett's own five-foot-ten, Brett always saw her as walking, talking spitfire. It was hard to imagine her as a college professor, which she was, in their old town of Alma.

"Is that another of your premonitions?" Brett asked. Madeline was a bit of a psychic and made quite a few cryptic remarks because of it. Of course, Brett didn't believe a word of it. But then again, just a few years ago she hadn't believed in ghosts either until she met one. Now she wasn't quite sure where she stood on the matter of ghosts. To the side, pretty much.

"No, it's a fact. The entire room will look entirely different once you finish bringing in the rest of the new furniture." Madeline returned to her work in the kitchen, leaving Allie to plot further machinations against Brett's sanity under Kurt's mischievous eye, or at least that was about what Brett made of it.

"Then let's just bring it all in and work it out from there."

"That would make entirely too much sense," Kurt said, swishing by. "I just *love* seeing you two all sweaty and butch!"

Brett looked at Frankie. "Fire extinguisher. Look into it." She headed back out to the truck to bring in more of the new furnishings, with Frankie following her.

"Yo, dude," Frankie said, "you brought this on yourself. With all the cheating and cyber-sexing it up and shit."

"Yeah, I know. I'm just hoping if I complain a bit, it'll get us off easier."

"So how're things with you two?"

Brett shrugged. "When we met, it was like this fierce heat, y'know?"

"Yeah, uh, well, I do get that, Brett. But I wasn't asking about then—I was asking about now."

Brett sat on the back of the truck. "She turns me on. I want her. I love making her come and scream my name and . . . well . . . Toblerone, dude. But see, I can't help taking a glance around sometimes, y'know?"

"Yeah, I got that. But Allie loves ya man, and if ya keep this shit up, she's gonna leave you. Whatchya gonna do then?"

"If she leaves me, she'll end up dating someone else, and I'll have to track them down and kill them. Quite simple, actually."

"But you forget you gone legit now."

"Only for Allie. If she leaves me, all bets are off."

"You can't do that, Brett. We agreed what side we're on now. And . . ." he trailed off, looking down.

"And what, Frankie?"

"And you saying that shit, well, it's like you're just trying to not make anything your fault. And that's just not right, Brett."

He was right. She was trying to deflect all blame for her actions. She was following in her familial path and doing just what they'd always done—make everything someone else's fault. And that it was Frankie doing such deep analysis was truly frightening. "Frankie, you're the one always on my side. And you getting into this psychological crap is . . . well it's scary as fuck."

"Yeah. I know. Sorry. It's Kurt and hanging out with you and Allie and Maddy and all that shit. Fuck, even Ski and Randi are doing it to me. I'm gonna be wearing Hawaii-type shirts and shorts next I know." He sat next to her.

"So pretty much, we're whipped. And we're fucked in all the wrong ways."

"Yeah."

"Remember the good old days, when I fucked who I wanted to, and you got blows from half the boys at the theater?"

Frankie tucked his thumbs into the waistband of his 505s. "Good times." He crossed his legs at the ankles. "But having somebody to pick up the groceries and make me eat something besides burgers and beer, now that's something that's really meaning something to me these days."

"So are you saying I could hire a maid and get all the same perks?"

"Most maids don't give bed service. They make 'em, not unmake 'em, y'know?"

"So I need a live-in maid and a live-in hooker?"

"Brett, we both done that life. We done it, lived it, bought the T-shirt, and sent it home to relatives. But y'know what? It can be fun. Enjoyable, even. But your maid and hooker won't care about you. Love you. They'll just be there to do what you tell 'em to."

"Sounds like a good deal to me."
"And you'll have to pay 'em."
"I got money."
"But, y'know, Brett . . . You keep getting—bringing—new women into your bed 'cause you're just trying to convince yourself you mean something. And Allie's the one who'll really do that for you. If you pay somebody, it won't mean jack."
"Frankie, dude, you are getting so close to insightful, it's downright scary as fuck."
"Yeah. It is. But you're playing these games for a reason, Brett. You're screwing with one of the best things your life has ever offered for a reason. Your family fucked you over and there's some things ain't ever gonna be right. You gotta get over it, dude."
"Okay, yeah, Frankie, you're right. Tell you what, you see me starting to step over the line, and you can smack me upside the head. You know me better'n anyone, so you'll see anything coming from a mile away."
"Yeah, but you'll just deny it all."
"Just smack me upside the head you think I'm up to no good, 'kay?"
"Will do. But you still gotta try to behave yourself, 'cause I can't be there twenty-four/seven, y'know?"
"Yeah Frankie, I know. And knowing you know ought to keep me honest. 'Kay?"
"Yeah. And Brett?"
"Yeah?"
"What's a Toblerone?"
Brett heard a gasp behind her just before she heard the slap of Allie's hand against her arm. "What have you been telling him?"
Great. Just what Brett needed—a trip to the doghouse just because she'd made a slight remark to Frankie. For fuck's sake, she didn't even tell him what it meant!

Chapter Two

Wednesday, 11:28 p.m.

That night at the bar, all of Frankie's insightfulness was still at the top of Brett's mind. She knew how true it all was. She knew how close she was to losing Allie. She'd already lost Allie once because she'd been dating Pamela Nelson, who danced at the Paradise Theater as Storm at the same time she'd first been seeing Allie. Allie had found out.

Just like Allie had recently found out Brett had been cyberring with a woman and ended up meeting that woman, spending the night with that woman. Even though Brett hadn't had sex with her, it had gotten complicated.

But then Brett had actually slept with Victoria (Pamela's younger sister), and well, there had been someone else Brett had slept with before, and Allie didn't know anything about either of those. As far as Brett was concerned, Allie could go to her grave not knowing anything Brett had done like that.

So Brett would behave. From now on. Really. Truly. Completely.

And overall, it pretty much scared her shitless to think about how much her familial relations guided her path—made her make the decisions she did. They had warped her in such a way that she figured she could do whatever she chose and use her past as an excuse.

Allie was the best thing that ever happened to her. She needed to make sure she didn't lose that. She had to do whatever was needed to preserve that.

But, oh, that cute blond was *so* flirting with her. Brett was willing to bet she'd cream her jeans at the slightest touch from . . . No. She had to concentrate on her woman. Allie. Her world.

But the girl was clearly trying to hook up with her. She was dancing provocatively while staring at Brett with her deep green eyes, keeping her arms over her head as she slowly wiggled her hips. She flipped her hair, thrust her breasts forward . . .

Brett allowed Allie to take her onto the dance floor, and she flicked her glance from the woman dancing for her and Allie. The music pulsed through her, and she broke out in a sweat.

Yeah, there was no doubt about it, the woman wanted Brett, and Brett knew it. And the music and alcohol pounding through her body made her want the woman, too, regardless of what she'd told—promised—Allie. And Frankie.

She spun on her heels, moving to the music, knowing she looked good. Even the mirrors testified to this. They reflected her lean, muscular frame, dark eyes, and black hair laced (just barely) with gray. She wore black leather jeans, boots, and a white T-shirt. The T-shirt showed off her arms, which were carved with muscle and not an ounce of fat. She was sweating just enough to give her hair a slightly damp look, making it layer just right. The boots she wore were perfect for dancing—their leather soles didn't cling to the floor at all, which allowed her the total body movement she enjoyed for dancing.

Allie, who was dancing across from her, looked pretty damned hot as well. Her simple blouse was just tight enough to reveal the swell of her breasts, and tight blue jeans flowed over her hips and down her long, long legs. Brown boots finished the look with heels that made her five foot nine height equal to Brett's. Her slender body, long blond hair, aristocratic features, and deep blue eyes had already attracted the attention of many women tonight.

Brett enjoyed that. She reveled in knowing her woman was attracting the attention of so many others because she knew who would be in Allie's bed that night. She also knew the alcohol of too many Miller Lites had given her a certain cockiness that made her very well aware of how many women were cruising her as well. And she loved every minute of it.

And, fuck, only a lot of alcohol would make her realize just how damned good she looked.

The song changed, briefly breezing through house music on its way to an older tune that Brett could really groove to. She flipped into her best "cool dude" image and fell to her knees in front of Allie, grabbing her girl around the waist as her hips pulsed to the beat.

Brett enjoyed these fast songs, songs she knew from her younger days, songs from the eighties, songs she could show off her body and its abilities. She liked showing off her moves, her flexibility as she knelt on the floor. She lowered herself so her back was on it before springing back up so Allie could dance and wriggle her way over her.

They danced well together.

She looked up at the screen where Olivia Newton-John, looking her very hottest with her body tightly clad in black spandex, looked down at her, singing about the one she wanted, then she looked over at the similarly blond Allie, with her smoldering looks, who met her gaze. She smirked, not allowing herself to show a full smile that would let on just how fucking happy she suddenly was.

Brett pulled her gaze from the random young hottie who wanted her and focused solely on her own hottie—Allie.

The Rainbow Room had always been one of Brett's favorite bars. These days Detroit had three primarily dyke bars—the Rainbow Room, Stilettos, and Sugarbaker's. Sugarbaker's was a sports bar, and Stilettos catered to a different crowd that was largely the diaper brigade and was located in the boonies as far as Brett was concerned. Normally on a Wednesday, nothing much happened at the Rainbow Room, but tonight, it was packed. And the Rainbow Room was Brett's bar of choice anyway. Not only was it her favorite, she could drive home drunk from there blindfolded, it was that close. To home. Her home. With Allie.

Brett danced up to Allie, pressing her leg between Allie's thighs and putting one hand on Allie's hip, pulling her close. Allie wrapped her arms around Brett's neck and grinned up at her before lowering her arms to cup Brett's ass and trace muscular thighs. Brett's other arm fell to her side. She knew her coolness, and she stuck by it, like a method actor did with a part.

Suddenly, Brett was hit across the back so hard that she fell forward into Allie.

"What the fuck?" Brett said, grabbing Allie to put her right on her feet and then whipping about to face their assailant. Wouldn't be good to go beating somebody while dropping Allie to the floor.

"Oh, shit, sorry—didn' see you standing there darlin'," the woman slurred, her eyes bleary in the multicolored disco globes. Her dark auburn hair fell over her shoulders and threatened to fall into her face as well. Although she was rather pretty, she was nearly anorexic. She half-disguised this with a bulky, light blue blazer. Brett couldn't believe she could wear such a thing in this heat.

"Yeah, whatever," Brett replied when Allie laid a gentle, restraining hand on her shoulder. She had to listen to Allie, had to make sure Allie knew how valued she was.

"Brett, let's go outside and get a breath of air, cool down a bit," Allie said, wiping a hand over her own sweat-drenched brow. Brett reluctantly followed her out to the patio, thankful when the cool night air caressed her overheated body. It was funny how inside, with the flying multicolored lights and music pounding not only in her ears, but up through her limbs and into her body from every available surface, Brett didn't really realize just how much she had to drink and how drunk she was.

It was also a wicked good way to get her anger up. Just walking outside made Brett feel ever so much calmer. The woman was just a crazy drunk who'd unintentionally bumped into her. No big.

Brett slipped her hand into her pocket for her smokes. She felt a piece of paper. She pulled it out. It was inscribed with a phone number and a cheerful *Call Me!* Brett had no doubt it was from the little hottie.

She smiled to herself.

Brett leaned against a table, her foot propped up on a chair. She was feeling pretty good with the breeze dancing through her hair, cooling her overheated system. Allie had run into a couple of old friends, and they sat at a table laughing and joking. Brett couldn't believe she'd almost lost it on that drunk inside. After all, the woman was just out having a good time—wasn't everyone?

Brett leaned back against one of the picnic tables and lit a cigarette, provocatively placing it between her lips while Allie sat looking up at her under the soft glow of the moonlight. A slow smile slid across Allie's face, and Brett knew she was getting lucky tonight. Hell, Brett would have taken Allie right there and then. She could imagine pressing Allie against the high, wooden privacy fence, pushing her leg between Allie's thighs, running her lips down Allie's neck and over that luscious collar bone, slowly pulling Allie's zipper down, reaching into her pants, under the elastic, feeling her wetness . . .

Instead, Brett took a deep breath and hit Allie with her best bedroom-eye gaze, stalking her like a jungle cat while slowly puffing on her smoke.

"Honey," Allie said, "would you mind getting us another round?"

"And I suppose you want me to buy as well," Brett replied with a quick grin before she got up and walked back into the bar, leaving the three laughing women behind her.

After fighting her way to the bar, she yelled her order to the cute bartender she liked, the one with the long, curly brown hair and open smile, then turned to wait for her drinks, glancing over at the dance floor to see if there were any interesting moves happening out there. Or any cute women.

She heard raised voices and saw a bit of a scuffle between the drunken woman of earlier and another brunette, this one with short dark hair. She looked like she could take care of herself, so Brett turned back to the bartender to collect her drinks. That was when, under the reds, blues, and purples of the disco globe almost hidden within the smoke the DJ was pouring onto the dance floor, she caught a glint of steel.

"Bitch!" a woman screamed.

Brett didn't think, she reacted. In just the flash she'd seen, she knew what the brunette had pulled, and she flew, taking the most direct route, leaping up and running across tabletops to the dance floor. Pushing aside several women who were just realizing what was happening, Brett grabbed the brunette's arm, her gun arm, and pushed it up. Brett shoved her other arm between the two women so that the drunk sailed backward onto the relative safety of the floor.

The woman with the gun—the brunette—tried to pull her arm back, and everyone around them screamed. Brett brought a leg behind the woman's shins and pushed her onto her back on the floor while they wrestled over the gun.

"Bitch!" the drunk screamed, trying to dive between Brett and the brunette.

Brett threw her off with one arm while she kept the gun-woman's hand pinned to the ground with her other arm. Several patrons pulled at her from behind, trying to get her off the brunette, but Brett wanted to get the gun out of the girl's hand first. The woman had her knee up in Brett's chest, trying to throw her off. Brett smashed the woman's arm against the floor till the gun skidded across the dance floor.

Both the drunk woman and Brett threw themselves toward it. Brett hated doing it, but she smashed the woman in the face with her fist when they reached the gun simultaneously. Brett rolled onto her back and quickly threw her hands over her head against the ground so she could throw herself back to her feet. She was ready to defend herself, but a pack of women were grabbing both the drunk and the brunette.

Brett emptied the bullets out of the gun into her hand. She put the bullets into her pocket and stuck the gun down the front of her jeans so no one could grab it.

"Rowan?" Allie said, looking from where she stood holding the drunk to where another woman stood holding the brunette. Allie returned to the bar when she heard the commotion. Rowan was an unusual name, Brett thought, and she recognized it from Allie's past. Allie once considered herself Rowan's mentor, and now, word was Rowan was a damned good cop.

A crowd gathered around them, including the bar's bouncers, who had been outside in the parking lot taking care of another problem. "Okay, okay, okay," one of them said. "We'll take it from here."

Rowan, the brunette with the gun, looked at Brett after the woman holding her let her go. "Look, I'm a cop—I need my gun back." She put her hand out expectantly.

"You pull a loaded gun in a public place when you're drinking, and you expect me to give it back to you?" Brett said, not quite believing anyone could be so idiotic.

A man and a woman, both fairly slender with brown hair, approached the group on the dance floor.

"I'm Jill's brother," the man said, indicating the drunken woman in the bouncer's arms. "We'll get her home and out of here. Sorry about any problems—it's her birthday, and I guess she had a few too many."

"Dave, I'm okay," Jill slurred, fighting the bouncers' grip on her. "It's just that . . . that . . . bitch—"

The woman with Dave grabbed Jill's arm and cut her off. "Jill, let's get gone, okay?"

Thankfully, Rowan kept her mouth shut during this interlude, until Dave and his girlfriend got Jill out of the bar.

"One of these days I'm gonna get that bitch, and good," Rowan said, staring toward the exit.

"Honey, just calm down, she didn't hurt anything," said a blond who stood next to her and laying a hand on her arm.

"Like hell she didn't—this bitch has my gun now!"

Before Brett could react, Allie anticipated her and jumped between them. "Rowan, calm down." She glanced around and noticed that things were returning to normal around them, but they were still in the middle of the dance floor. "Let's go outside."

The moonlight no longer seemed quite so enchanting out on the patio. Brett leaned against a table, sipping her Miller Lite from the bottle while puffing on a Marlboro. Rowan's gun was still in the front of her pants. She was surprised the bouncers hadn't taken it from her, but Rowan showing off her badge probably convinced them otherwise.

"Anytime we're anywhere, and she's there, she's causing a problem," the blond, who identified herself as Lauren, said. On this rather warm night, she was wearing shorts and a sports bra, showing off nicely tanned stomach and legs.

"If she had been a better girlfriend in the first place, she wouldn't have lost you," Rowan grumbled.

"What I don't believe," Allie said, putting her hands on her shapely hips, "is that I run into an old friend after years apart and all you can do is bitch about your girlfriend's ex?" A smile danced across her full lips.

"I'm sorry, hon," Rowan said, giving Allie a big hug and lifting her right off the ground.

Brett gave them a few moments then felt obligated to remind them of her presence. "Umm, I think that's enough."

"Oh, Rowan," Allie said, stepping back and into Brett's arms. "This big, bad bulldyke is my girlfriend." She was obviously in a teasing mood tonight. Perhaps Brett should do some teasing of her own when they got home.

On their way home Allie filled Brett in on some of the little drama played out by Rowan, her girlfriend Lauren, and Lauren's ex, Jill. Apparently, this tango had been going on in various permutations for quite a while.

From everything Allie had ever heard, it didn't surprise her that Jill would toy with her brother and his girlfriend and bring them to the Rainbow Room for her birthday. It was also predictable that she'd try to make the moves on Lauren after she'd had a few. Hell, it didn't even seem as if she needed to drink anything to make the moves on the cute blond.

As it turned out, Rowan had first begun her career as a cop back in Southfield, working with Allie for a while. Brett didn't like the fact that some cops thought they could get away with anything—from speeding, to drinking and driving, to just plain stupid behavior. Like bringing a gun into a bar—oh, and then pulling it out. Back in the old days, Brett usually armed herself, but she wouldn't have drawn it for such a ridiculous reason, not in public, not for something so inane. She usually only drew her weapon when someone else pulled theirs, or if she knew they'd be pulling it soon.

Some people used a gun to make them feel big. Brett already knew her own strength and power. After all, she wasn't exactly short shit.

"What are you brooding about over there?" Allie asked with a teasing smile.

Brett glanced at Allie and thought guiltily of the woman who'd been flirting with her—and how she'd flirted back. How could she have even considered fooling around with anyone else while she had this incredible woman willing to be with her?

When they got home, they were barely inside the door when Brett pulled Allie up against her. Allie kissed Brett—hard and hungry—her soft hand at the back of Brett's head, tangled in her hair, urgently demanding Brett to deepen the kiss, to delve her tongue farther into her.

Brett pushed Allie back against a wall, putting her leg between Allie's. Her hands started around Allie's waist and then traveled down over her hips to caress her ass.

She wanted this woman, needed her. The smell of Allie overwhelmed her—the mixture of musky perfume, clean skin and hair, mousse, dryer sheets and detergent from her clothes. At times the entire Allie smell comforted Brett, while at other times like these, it turned her on.

She buried her face in Allie's hair, inhaling deeply. She kissed Allie's neck, running her tongue up the tender skin to her ear where she circled the lobe, working her way around the small diamond stud and gold hoop Allie wore in two piercings in each ear.

Allie moaned and squirmed against Brett when Brett's tongue dove inside her ear, gently teasing. Brett could feel the warmth of Allie's breath against her neck, the softness of her breasts against her own. She paused for a moment, laying her head on Allie's shoulder, then she looked up and into the depths of Allie's eyes. "I love you." Allie smiled, took Brett's hands in her own, leaned forward and kissed her. "Let's go upstairs."

"You go on ahead, I'll be up in a moment," Brett said. She watched Allie leave, went to the stereo, selected Chico Debarge's *Long Time No See*, and put it on.

Upstairs in the bedroom, Allie hadn't turned on any lights. Instead she had lit candles around the room, giving it a dreamlike quality. When Brett entered, Allie was bent over, lighting the last one on the bedside table.

Brett walked up behind her, wrapping her arms around her.

Allie stood and leaned back into the embrace. Brett kissed her neck and used her hands to trace lines down Allie's front, over her plush breasts, down her flat stomach, and over her hips.

She pushed herself tighter against Allie, wanting to feel her, meld with her, become one with her. She unbuttoned Allie's shirt, gently tugging it from her jeans, then reached up and deftly undid the front clasp on her bra.

Allie moaned when Brett took her breasts into her hands, gently pinching the hardened nipples. "Oh, God, Brett, I want to feel you inside me."

Brett finished undressing Allie, and Allie helped her to undress. Brett picked Allie up and put her on the bed, covering her body with her own, warmth on warmth.

Their lips again met, their tongues dancing with each other inside the union of their mouths. Allie pushed up against Brett's thigh, which was again between her own. Brett could feel the wetness of Allie's arousal against her skin.

Their bodies were molded together with nothing separating them, their curves entwined as one, each pushing against the other, trying to get even closer still so that nothing would part them. Brett couldn't get close enough even though it felt as if they were already one—two souls united in one body, or two bodies united with one soul. Allie's heat seeped into her, she could feel her heartbeat in her own heart, and their gasping breaths were as one.

She slowly kissed her way down Allie, tasting the salt of her sweat, teasing her nipples, nibbling gently around the navel ring, with Allie squirming beneath her all the while. She made her way down the incredibly long length of Allie's legs until she could nibble and suck gently on Allie's toes.

"Brett, please, you're driving me crazy," Allie moaned. But Brett wanted to drive Allie crazy, wanted to taste and touch each of the places that drove her nuts before taking her the rest of the way. The buildup was half the fun and going crazy made it all the more worthwhile. Brett loved making Allie scream, but she also loved making her squirm and giving her pleasure upon pleasure.

She sucked her inner thighs, kissed the spot on the back of her neck, licked between her shoulder blades, and tongued her navel before finally brushing her chin against her cunt and gently tasting her with her tongue.

Allie was drenched, and Brett first ran her tongue up and down slowly, then went inside of her with her tongue, fully feeling and tasting her before inserting first one, then two, then three fingers into her while she licked the swollen flesh of her clit.

Brett coated her hand with Allie's own juices, then slowly inserted the rest of her fist, still working her tongue over Allie's pussy, beating the hardened clit back and forth.

"Oh, God, Brett," Allie said, writhing across the bed.

Brett could feel her insides, could feel her warmth, and felt a part of her. She moved her fist around, clenching and unclenching.

"Brett . . . Brett . . . Brett!"

Brett hung on while Allie whipped her around the bed.

Chapter Three

Thursday, 9:12 a.m.

When Brett was in junior high and high school, she worked multiple jobs to make sure she could get out of her house, away from all of her family's failures and go to college, even if she couldn't get a scholarship. She was willing to do anything to ensure that once high school was done, she'd never have to see her family again. On the other side, though, she wanted to show them all—all those teachers who never thought she'd amount to anything, the other kids who grew up around her who harassed and beat her up, as well as her drunken, violent, and abusive family.

But to do all that, she'd had to keep her own name so they'd know. When she was on the lam, she had to live under an alias, but she was happy to reclaim it just so she could, if she wanted, track down those bastards she was supposed to call family and rub their faces in it—let them see how she had made it, how she had moved beyond the legacy of fear and hate she had been raised into.

To Brett's sleep-drenched mind, the smell of food cooking squirmed into her dreams as a Mickey D's breakfast she was cooking when she was working in one in high school . . .

Brett was swimming in a sea of sleep, trying to reach up and out. She was aware of Allie's soft body lying next to her own, aware of the sweet smell of Allie's hair surrounding her face. She drifted back to sleep with a smile on her face, but there was something else—the smell of coffee, bacon, and eggs drifting up the staircase from the first floor.

Brett opened her eyes slightly and saw that the sun was already up. She glanced at the clock and realized she should get up even though they'd closed the bar the night before. But Brett was of the firm opinion that "good morning" was one of the world's greatest oxymorons. Mornings wouldn't be quite so bad if they came far later in the day.

She lifted her head from the satin pillowcase and sniffed again, this time with her eyes open, before dropping her head back onto the pillow. Shit. She just knew it was Madeline. Maddy probably had some sort of premonition or read some tea leaves or dog shit or . . . Damn. Maddy, a professor at Alma College, and her girlfriend Leisa, a high school teacher, were on summer break and decided to spend it at Brett's. They had already made themselves at home and this made Brett worry that they'd be hanging around way more this summer than she liked.

Brett pulled on her green and black bathrobe and her matching Pooh Bear slippers. They were a Christmas present from Allie who had explained that Pooh was the perfect counterpoint to her big bad ass image. She padded down the stairs, following the delightful smells of breakfast.

Most people would have greeted Brett with a cheery "good morning" or with a small remark about the weather and food. Not Madeline Jameson. Maddy looked up at Brett and said, "You won't be able to help it, you know."

Brett glanced at Leisa.

Leisa shrugged, buttering toast and slicing it diagonally. "I still don't understand. All I know is it's summer break, and she made me get up at seven to come down here for some sort of emergency."

Brett stared at the two for a moment, watching Maddy flip the bacon and sausages in a pan. When Brett was certain no further unprompted words of wisdom were to follow, she grabbed the coffee pot and poured herself a mug.

"I hope you like it, it's French vanilla. I also picked up some regular cream and some Irish cream," Maddy said.

"Uh-huh."

Madeline handed Brett a plate piled high with sunny-side up eggs, sausage links, and bacon. Leisa plopped two pieces of toast onto the corner of the plate. They knew Brett too well.

Brett lightly sprinkled salt and pepper on her eggs, cut off the whites, and ate those first with the sausage while Madeline cracked two more eggs into the pan.

Allie came down a few minutes later. "Mmm, something smells good." Madeline handed Allie a plate with the eggs over easy and just bacon, extra crispy, and just one slice of toast. Allie grabbed a cup of coffee and joined Brett at the table.

Leisa poured orange juice for all of them. "Need the vities," she said. Brett guessed she meant the vitamins. Leisa put together her own plate, and Maddy followed suit.

Maddy sat next to Leisa. "Allison, dear, would you please help me explain to Brett that she simply will not be able to remain uninvolved?"

Allie stopped with her fork midway to her mouth. "Umm, uninvolved in what?"

Madeline gave a little wave of her hand. "Uninvolved in whatever it is that's going on." She looked at Brett.

"Ya got me," Brett explained to Allie, mopping up the rest of the yolk with a piece of toast.

"I don't know exactly what it is that is going on," Madeline said. "But I do know that Brett is trying to appear disinterested, opposed even. But her involvement is necessary because she knows what it is to be wrongly accused."

"Oh, that's happened a few times, hasn't it Brett?" Leisa said.

Brett looked at Allie and shrugged.

"When will you two ever realize that I do not need the details in order to understand something?" Madeline inquired. "If you must be tied so to the tangible plane, then why don't you fill me in on the specifics of the matter." It wasn't really a question, but not an order, either.

Brett took her plate to the sink. "I'm really just clueless. No idea what you're on about."

Brett walked into the Paradise Theater later thinking about lots of different things. It was funny to think that the Paradise she was now walking into wasn't the original one, instead a rebuilt one. It seemed so much like the original—the turnstiles and division of auditoriums were exactly the same. Hell, everything was exactly the same.

To the left was the gay side of the theater where gay male movies played nonstop and male strippers did their thing on Friday and Saturday nights. In the eighties, male strippers danced every night, but the advent of VCRs changed the adult business—openly gay men bought porno flicks to watch at home. Only married men came to the theater. After all, they couldn't watch them at home with the little missus around. And those men feared being seen and recognized when the lights came on to spotlight and show dancers.

Men also went to the gay side of the Paradise for a little illicit action. At the back of the auditorium there was a large, dark room, with a bathroom, just before the back exit. Without looking, Brett knew that the floor there would be sticky and littered with condoms, even though they had a maintenance man who cleaned and mopped the entire theater each day with bleach.

To the right was the straight side. Along the walls leading to the ticket window were pictures of the girls dancing this week with signs that said, "Admission: $10 Couples: $17." The showtimes, five times a day, were also listed.

This was the way Brett entered the theater, just as she had

almost every day for the first eight years she'd worked there the first time around and now for the past several years.

But she'd always know the place by the smell alone. No matter what they did to keep it clean, no matter how much they scrubbed and tried to get the dancers to cooperate, regardless of the cleansing ritual of fire that had taken it down, the smell was still there, almost a palpable entity by itself. There was the smoke from cigars, pipes, thousands of cigarettes, and more than a few joints. All this mingled with the smell of sweat and unwashed bodies, the lingering odor from women wearing far too much perfume, and, of course, the ever-present odor of come.

Brett remembered working there in her early days. She hadn't questioned how many condoms she sold to the guys on the straight side. She just assumed the dancers were doing slightly more full-service lap dances than they were legally allowed. But one day Rick, the owner and her boss, explained that the men didn't want to splooge their clothes, so they wore the condoms while they jerked off watching the dancers and movies. They didn't want their filthy and telltale come to give away how they spent their time.

Many people might have been surprised, but it didn't shock Brett at all to discover she felt like she had finally come home. Except . . . except all of that was before Allie. All of that was who she was then, instead of what she was now. She breathed in the filth, studied the sleazy pictures on the walls and toed the dead body of a mouse that had crawled into a corner prior to its demise.

Using her key, she went through the door instead of the turnstile and headed for the box office through which the upstairs offices were accessed.

She remembered one night when the clerk passed out in the box office, and two of the dancers broke down the door. The interesting thing was that those particular dancers were probably the only two who would've done what they did—they didn't touch a cent of the money in the cash register. Instead they just wanted to ring in more customers because it was to their advantage to have as many johns in the audience as possible.

She nodded to the clerk and unlocked the door that led upstairs.

When Frankie tried to talk her into coming back to work at the Paradise, he had outfitted an office for her and had done it well. The walls were a cream-colored, textured tint, the floors real hardwood with a deep green Oriental rug, and the walls were accented by two of her favorite Ansel Adams prints. The large desk, credenza, bookshelves, and bar were all a deep, rich oak. Her chair, the couch, and two visitors' chairs were upholstered in dark leather and set in oak frames. She liked leather and wood. Real wood—not pressboard and definitely not mod-deco-metal stuff.

She pulled out a Marlboro Light and a Zippo, the one Allie had given her. She went to the window and looked out at the potholed street and broken pay phones. Across Woodward was a still-operating convenience store with boarded up windows. One day she had been standing at this very window when she realized someone was mugging a nun across the street. She stood and watched it for a moment before realizing she had it wrong—the nun was mugging someone. And then, just as she was thinking maybe she ought to go downstairs and do something about it, the muggee hit the nun upside the head with something so Brett could see it wasn't a nun doing the mugging, it was some dude dressed up as a nun. She had figured he deserved what he got and let the muggee beat the crap outta him.

She grabbed a can of Diet Pepsi from the fridge and glanced at her watch. Almost eleven. She usually got in around ten, but flex time was one of the perks of being the boss.

The dancers were already at work, and music was pumping through the building, coming up through the floorboards from the auditorium below. She flipped the switch on the power strip for her computer. She spent the next several hours reviewing the budgets and timelines for some of their upcoming projects. The phone rang. She reached over and hit the speakerphone. "Hello."

"Hey honey." It was Allie. Her voice covered Brett like a warm cloak. "How's it going?" Brett detected a strain in her tone.

"Tell the truth, my bloody head feels like it's about to explode. I've been working with spreadsheets all day today."

"Well . . . I hate to be a bother, but I was wondering if you could do me a favor?"

"Whatcha need babe?"

Allie took a deep breath. "Jill, that woman who caused all those problems at the bar, was murdered last night."

"What?"

"Somebody broke into her house in the middle of the night and shot her. Her brother Dave found the body this morning. She lives . . . lived in Ferndale. So it's Ferndale's case."

"And you're calling me about this because . . . ?"

"The police arrested Rowan. Apparently they found out about the fight at the bar and the bad blood between Rowan and Jill."

"And again, I'm not tracking."

Allie sighed. "The Ferndale police are pretty much not saying anything about it at all to the Detroit cops, since Rowan's a Detroit cop now. Randi thought maybe you might be able to help us out."

"Hold on. Randi can't find out anything. Ski can't find out anything." Ski, or Joan Lemanski, was a Lansing detective and Randi's girlfriend. "So you're asking me if *I* can find out anything?"

"Yeah. That's about the size of it. Ferndale says they don't want a bunch of extra cops running around messing things up. They're already pretty . . . Well."

"What do you know so far?"

"They arrested her. Rowan. She tested positive on the paraffin test—showing that she had recently fired a gun. And her gun, which incidentally matched the bullets found in Jill and her house, had been fired recently."

"Sorry to say, Al, but it sounds pretty open and shut to me."

"Yes, I know. And some other people seem to think so, too."

"What do you mean?" Brett asked, looking out her window just in time to see a mugging in progress. It wasn't anyone she knew.

"Brett, we all know that cops behind bars aren't really safe. Not only do the guards resent their presence, but the other cons . . . She got away."

"Got away? What do you mean she got away?"

"From the police station. She was about to be booked and . . . she got away. Another cop, or maybe several, must've helped her, knowing how bad it looked for her and how she'd get treated in the lockup and all."

"Oh, shit, man. Allie, even if the woman isn't guilty, which is a slim-to-none chance if you ask me, then this sure as hell makes it look like she is."

"Brett, I'm not sure of a whole lot right now, but one of the few things I am sure about is that I don't really need your interpretation of things at the moment. Another thing I know is that I have to help Rowan."

"Allie—"

"Brett, we were partners."

It didn't take much for Brett to fill in the blanks. She knew about debts like this. She might not understand a lot about Allie being a cop, but she could understand partners. For instance, Brett would do anything for Frankie. Quite simply, you watched your partner's back and vice versa. Even if you weren't partners any more. "What do you need me to do?"

Allie paused. Brett knew she was going through a lot right then. "Do you guys have anybody from Ferndale on the payroll?"

"Um, Allie, just where are you calling me from?"

There was a pause while Allie realized exactly what Brett meant. "Oh, shit. I'm calling you from home." Just what Brett needed, her lover implicating her over the phone in bribery or something worse. Obviously, Brett needed to have a talk with Allie about *not* discussing illegal activities over the phone. Allie should have known better, Brett thought.

"Then you know the answer already. But, regardless, I think it would be the same no matter where you were calling me from."

"Well, could you try to think of anything? Find out anything?"

Brett smiled. "Yeah, I will. I love you." She put down the phone and called out, "Frankie!" His office was next to hers, and they were the only two who worked up here now.

"Yeah, boss. Whatcha need?" When he'd rebuilt the Paradise, he'd made sure all the doorways could accommodate his massive six-foot-four frame. Today he was wearing a black suit, black shoes, a white shirt, and a thin black tie. His thick, wavy black hair looked recently cut, and his suit and shirt were neatly pressed. Obviously, his new love was having an effect on him. But Brett couldn't help but wonder if he'd been watching *Pulp Fiction* again.

"Do we got anybody from Ferndale on payroll?"

"Shit, no. Why would we need that? I mean, we used to have a few guys there, but even then it wasn't really necessary." Ferndale was located between Royal Oak and Detroit, lying right on the Eight Mile boundary that marked Detroit's northernmost points. It was a bedroom community that was again becoming a hotspot ever since the gays had started moving in, renovating, and increasing property values. Ferndale, an older community, was now a very gay-friendly place. In fact, on their city marquee, which stood right at the corner of Nine Mile and Woodward, they frequently advertised the goings-on of the local LesBiGay group called FANS of Ferndale. Brett always wondered what FANS stood for.

Most of Brett's and Frankie's operations took place in Detroit and were legal. Mostly. Any adult business wasn't likely to keep strictly on the right side of the law, so it always paid to keep a few of the local force on payroll. And maybe a few judges as well. But Brett and Frankie did business in Motown, and that's where they invested their cash.

"Whatcha need, anyway?" Frankie asked.

"Well, a friend of Allie's got fingered for a murder that happened there, and I guess the Ferndale cops are locking out Detroit 'cause Rowan's Detroit PD."

Frankie let out a hearty chuckle. "Leave it to the cops to shut down on their own kind. A cop wouldn't know a friend if they was introduced."

"Maybe they do, Frankie. Someone helped Rowan escape. She's nowhere to be found."

"Huh. I'll see if I can find anybody if you want."

"That'd be great, Frankie. I'm sure Allie'd really appreciate it."

Brett spent the rest of the day doing various business analyses and working with some budgets. Frankie brought Brett back into the biz to help build it back up and beyond what Rick DeSilva had made of it. Only this time they were doing it all legally. For the most part.

They had decided against having anything to do with the drug trade, but the Internet and technology had opened myriad possibilities that hadn't been available in Rick's time. Brett wanted to take advantage of them all.

Initially she figured they'd explore one or two additional revenue streams, but then she realized there weren't any published industry trends to track for her analyses and few places to mine for business development information to determine what areas would be ripe for expansion. She settled on trying a few at a time, based on potential risks and gains and other things she was feeling her way through.

Of course, such well-laid plans required some patience, and she wasn't big with that.

Chapter Four

Thursday, 6:36 p.m.

When Brett got home from work she found Allie and Madeline discussing what Brett now called "the Rowan situation." Because she came in through the side door, they didn't hear her enter.

"Madeline," Allie was saying from her seat on the living room sofa, "I don't know what I'm going to do. I have to help Rowan, I know she didn't do it, but no one in Ferndale's talking, and I can't find out anything from anyone else."

"Allison, if she is indeed innocent, then her innocence will speak for itself."

"What we need to do is brainstorm," Leisa said. "That's what we did when Brett had her . . . um . . . problems . . . and it really helped. We have to break this down: What do we need, what do we need to do, et cetera. Maybe a whiteboard would help?"

"I prefer easels with those new Post-it pads," Brett said, entering the room. "How 'bout we just sit down and talk this out, eh?"

Madeline turned toward Brett. "Sometimes when you seek the solution to a problem, the answer is not as far away as you imagine."

Brett stared at Madeline for a moment, then turned to Allie. "Huh?"

Brett definitely knew how criminal minds worked, after all she herself possessed one. She also knew about honoring one's obligations. Most of all, she knew how to investigate. Maybe Madeline wasn't as crazy as she sometimes appeared.

"I don't know how to begin helping Rowan," Allie said. "We haven't been able to figure anything out all day. All we have is online news and what little Randi's been able to uncover, and it isn't all that helpful."

Brett snickered. "Whaddya expect from her? The good stuff?" When Brett and Allie broke up for a while several years before, Allie had dated Randi, a Detroit detective with the department's organized crime team. Brett hated Randi for that ever since, and the feeling was mutual.

It didn't help that Randi was still in love with Allie. The fact that Randi started dating Joan Lemanski, or Ski, a Lansing police detective last year, did help the situation. They really did have rather complicated lives.

"From what I've heard, you couldn't come up with anything more," Leisa said.

"Well, um, let's see, I was asked if I had anybody from Ferndale on my payroll, and I don't, so . . ." Brett walked over to the liquor cabinet and poured herself two fingers of Glenfiddich. "I figured if Allie needed anything more, she'd ask. I did double-check, made sure we didn't have anyone there, and we didn't. So I just did my work and went on with the day."

Allie looked at Brett and wondered why Brett hadn't thought to really help her with her current situation. Allie was always helping

Brett, so why didn't it work both ways? "Brett, she saved my life. She took a bullet for me. I owe her something. I have to help her."

"We need to figure out what to do next," Leisa said.

"First they lock us out of the situation, then they let her take off running." Brett said, sitting next to Allie and tossing an arm around her. "They probably thought they were helping."

"She's a cop," Allie stated. "They know there're lots of us willing to go to almost any lengths to protect her while all they want to do is find the truth. And we all know what it's like for a cop behind bars."

"Perhaps we need to define who *they* are," Maddy said.

"There *are* quite a few pronouns lying about," Leisa said.

"Listen." Allie stood, literally stamped her foot and addressed Brett directly. "*We* saw what happened last night. *We* were there. What I want to know is how her gun got fired, how she tested positive on the paraffin test, why her fingerprints were in Jill's house, and why the bullets match hers!"

"Perhaps she did indeed perpetrate the crime," Madeline said. "Passion and alcohol can be a very potent mix. As an ex-police officer, Allie, you must have seen it before."

"You don't know Rowan. There has to be a logical explanation for it all," Allie said.

"She had no goddamned business shooting that gun last night, and we all know it," Brett said. "She was drunk. She shouldn't have even had the gun with her at the bar."

"I'm sensing you might have some issues," Maddy said, looking at Brett.

"Cops can get away with so much shit just 'cause they're cops. It pisses me off," Brett said.

"We need to find her," Allie said, ignoring Brett. "We need to find Rowan and figure out what really happened. Lauren's frantic. She says Rowan was with her all night, but she's her lover, so—"

"So the cops might just discount that alibi." Brett finished for her. "Why the hell did she run? She has to know how that looks!" Already tired of it all, Brett went into the kitchen and inspected the contents of the fridge.

"She's innocent. She ran because she knew how it looked. I wouldn't be surprised if we end up finding her around here somewhere, trying to figure out who did it herself," Allie said.

"You know, as far as I know, nothing has ever been known to magically appear in a refrigerator regardless of how long you gaze into its depths," Madeline said to Brett.

Brett looked at Allie. No wonder Ferndale wanted all other cops locked out of the case—they'd merely interfere and get in the way. The one thing Brett knew for certain was that she would've run, too, had she been Rowan.

Brett looked at the women. "Do you have any idea how quickly Allie would arrest Rowan herself if she didn't know her?"

"Yes. I do," Madeline replied. That was it. No argument, no strange logic, or mystical messages. Madeline just got up and started making dinner.

"Aren't you going to say anything else?" Allie said in amazement.

"No. Why should I?" Madeline turned toward her. "You already know what I'd say if I were to say it."

"Okay, I give. Could you fill me in?" Brett asked.

"Rowan left, she ran. Her fingerprints were in Jill's house, her gun had been recently fired, and the bullets from it match those in Jill. Her hands had traces that show she recently fired a gun—"

"You know what I mean."

Madeline looked at her. "Brett. There's a reason Leisa and I are here. And it's not because we're on summer break. I love you both like . . . like we might have been lovers in past lives. We are connected, we four." Suddenly Brett felt as if she were a small child at her feet. "You know what you must do, and, for all that I know, my role is simply to help you do what you must, for you fear it."

"I fear it?" Yeah, right, Brett thought.

"You know what your role is within your limited concept of right and wrong, good and evil. Within your universe, you know where you stand. Yet, there is much more than that."

"Right and wrong, good and evil? Maddy, are you nuts? I know where I stand—I'm the bad guy wearing the black hat!"

"But that is merely your perception of yourself, not necessarily the reality of the matter." Madeline gazed at her through the steam of the sauté and vegetables. "It's rather like a cat having three names—one is cat, another is that by which a person names it, and the third, and most important, is that by which the cat calls itself. You play the role that others expect you—that of the first two, thus disregarding the latter, that by which you know yourself."

"Madeline, I might understand you a bit better if you talked in English," Brett said.

"I am speaking the language you know," Maddy said, tapping Brett's chest, "deep down inside of you, within that part you hide from everybody except Allie. And even to her you only show that part while cloaked in the darkness of night. You hide yourself within that version, that role, that you think people want you to portray, whilst underneath it all, you do what you believe is right and good."

Allie wrapped her arms around Brett from behind. "Brett. I need your help. I need to help Rowan. She didn't do it."

"And how do you know that?"

"She's a cop."

"And cops don't go bad?"

"Not Rowan. Brett, she saved my life—took a bullet for me. She was my partner. She was my Frankie."

After dinner, Brett sat on the front porch smoking a pipe and watching the rollerbladers skate by. Sixth Street was the best street in Royal Oak to skate with its recent repaving.

Dammit, Brett thought to herself, this was supposed to be her happily-ever-after, and it didn't seem too happy at the moment.

Almost on cue, the screen door opened and closed behind her, and Brett felt Allie's warmth against her back. Allie wrapped an arm around her neck. She felt Allie's soft breasts pressed against her back and couldn't help but lean into the softness.

"So you'll help?" Allie whispered into her ear, her lips just brushing Brett's earlobe.

"As if that was ever a question," Brett said, still watching the street. She was pretty sure a couple of dykes lived in the yellow house just kitty-corner from them. "Maddy had it down—I just had to blow some smoke."

Allie brushed her lips lightly over Brett's ear. "I know. But thank you anyway."

Brett stood and pulled Allie into her arms. "Aw, heck, it's the least I can do, what with everything," she whispered into the silky locks of Allie's hair. She stepped back, one arm circling Allie's waist, the other exploring the softness of her face. No matter what was ever said or not said, done or not done, she loved this woman through to the end. "What do you need me to do?"

Allie led her by the hand back inside. "Right now, I pretty much just need your criminal mind."

"Well, that's different."

"We need to develop a plan of action," Madeline said, sitting in the living room.

"And I'm plan girl?" Brett said.

"You're plan girl," Leisa said. "Like the way you orchestrated all of that tailing and chasing and stuff in Lansing last year. You could probably direct a play or something. Hey, do you want to help me direct the school play or put together the talent show next year?"

"You're insane," Brett said. "Now, why don't we go through what we know so I can really get a good picture of it all?" She went to the study to grab a notebook and pen. "So why don't we take it from the top? What do we know, and how do we know it?" She sprawled out on the love seat along the far wall of the room. Maddy and Leisa lounged on the sofa, and Allie paced the room.

"The evidence is piled against Rowan," Allie said. "But it's so complete and total that it's just like . . . well, one of the situations you get yourself into, Brett, where you have to wonder if the only reason it's piled that high is because someone else set it up as a frame."

"Or else it could be that she's . . . uh . . . guilty?" Brett said.

"Hey, we're here to get her off," Leisa said.

"There's no getting off," Allie said. "She's not guilty. We're here to prove that and to find out who really did it."

"By calling her guilty, I'm making us really look at the situation from all sides and angles," Brett said. "What do we know?"

"Okay, so Dave and Diane took Jill to the bar that night," Allie said, pacing. "It was Jill's birthday, and so she got to choose what they did, where they went. Apparently Jill liked messing with Dave and Diane, so she wanted to take them to a gay restaurant and then a gay bar. Her dinner was at La Dolce Vita, and then they went to the Rainbow Room. She told Dave to be glad she didn't go with her evil thoughts and make them take her to a fag bar where Dave might get hit on and such."

"And how do you know all this?" Brett asked.

"Randi. Because Rowan's a cop, some bits and pieces got down there," Allie said. "Randi was able to find out some things."

"So, it's all pretty much rumor and conjecture," Brett said.

Allie ignored her. "Dave was supposed to help Jill move some things, so he showed up at her place before he went in to work today. She didn't answer, so he used his key, because he has one, being her brother and all, and let himself in. He called the police as soon as he found her."

Brett knew well the smells of death—the stench of blood and bodily fluids as the body gives up its life and control. Then there was the unavoidable odor of rotting flesh, even though Jill had only been dead a few hours at the most in an air-conditioned house.

"Apparently Dave was convinced it was a homophobic thing," Allie said. "But then he mentioned the argument at the bar last night, just one occurrence in a long-running feud between a Detroit cop and his sister, and all the attention turned to Rowan."

"Shortly after she was arrested and locked up, she cleverly escaped," Maddy added with a grin.

"But they had compiled an astonishing list of evidence against her first," Leisa said.

"As mentioned earlier," Allie said, "she had fired a gun, her gun had been fired, and her bullets matched those in the corpse."

"And yet you're convinced she's innocent?" Brett asked. She leaned back with her pipe and cupped its hand-carved bowl in the curve of her fingers.

"Yes," Allie replied, without hesitation. "You don't know Rowan like I do."

"Allie, we all know that by the time I could do anything, we'd already be starting a day late and, correct me if I'm wrong here, but aren't most murders solved within forty-eight hours if they're ever solved at all?" Brett knew a few things, and she'd never give Allie this opening if she wasn't absolutely certain of her facts, because this was Allie's field, not hers.

"And then you must realize that seventy-five percent of murder victims are male, and ninety percent of the defendants are male, so this situation is already abnormal," Allie paused, not breaking eye contact. "Rowan started out with me in Southfield. She saved my life one night when we went to investigate a residential complaint. There was a suspicious fellow lurking around. What we didn't know was he had friends there. I was prepared for the first one, but when the other two came out of the building shooting . . ." Allie trailed off, staring toward the shelf in the corner as she remembered that night. Brett could imagine. She could picture Rowan diving to pull Allie out of the way, see the two of them rolling on the ground with their guns pulled.

Brett reached over and wrapped an arm around Allie. She picked up her Scotch, swirled it around in the glass so the ice clinked, and propped her feet on the coffee table. "I'm in. There's gotta be something the coppers are overlooking and shit. Tell me more."

Chapter Five

Thursday, 10:00 p.m.

"Don't take no offense on this," Brett said, "but I'd like to start with why we've got Maddy and Leisa and *not* Randi and Ski here. After all, Randi and Ski would be likely to be of a bit more help in this situation."

"Ski doesn't know anyone down here," Allie said.

"Plus," Leisa said, "she had some hot new case and couldn't get away."

"Randi had a stakeout tonight," Allie said. "She couldn't get away, and it's not like she was Rowan's partner or anything. She wants to help, but she already knows she can't do much, being locked out and all."

"Not really anything at all," Leisa said.

"Okay, so what do we know about the sitch?" Brett asked. "I'm looking for a bit more detail, backstory, exposition—whatever you've got, really."

"I'm not real sure about everything that went on with Lauren and Jill," Allie said. "Lauren, the woman who was with Rowan last night, was apparently Jill's first love. They were together quite a while, but broke up during college—"

"Enter Rowan," Madeline said, apparently sensing where this was going.

"Hold on," Leisa said. "*Together quite a while*? What, did they hook up in elementary school?"

Allie ignored Leisa. "Rowan and Lauren got together, and Jill's never forgiven them."

"Sounds more like Jill'd have a reason to take care of Rowan, not vice versa," Brett said, her arm along the back of the loveseat.

"The motivations of the human character have mystified artists for centuries," Madeline said. "The intricacies of our condition, of our lives, provide endless variations for those who do, to do."

Brett looked at Madeline. "So what you're saying is this is one big, fucking mess, eh?"

Madeline looked deep into her eyes, ceasing all other movement in the room. "That is exactly what I am saying."

That night, with the moon shining through the windows, Allie awoke, pulled herself out of the security of Brett's strong arms, threw on a robe and went downstairs. She took out an old photo album, gingerly glancing over pictures of her and Rowan and Rowan and Lauren, remembering the old days, when she had worked with Rowan, before she had gotten back together with Brett and went on the lam with her.

Years ago, she'd never have guessed where her life would take her.

For instance, when she was young, she would not have believed she'd grow up to be gay. And a cop. And involved in a murder. Actually, several now, but she was far more comfortable thinking about other things, so she thought about school.

She had gone back to school, taking classes to help her figure out what she wanted to be when she grew up. Her courses were interesting, but her women's studies classes drove a wedge between her and Brett. They were making her look at Brett and Brett's work in a not-so-nice way. Porn just was not her thing. No matter what she saw, heard, and learned, she'd never fully understood why women did such things to themselves.

But she was a cop. A detective. That was who she was, and when she admitted it to herself, the women's studies classes were annoying her—not so much the classes as the women in them. So much of it was about being more PC than thou. And when her car was in the shop and Brett had to pick her up . . .

"Hey, babe," Brett said, walking up behind her and wrapping her arms around Allie's waist. Brett looked up at Allie's friends. "Hey, girls."

"We're not girls," Lessa said.

"Aren't we butch?" Leah teased Brett.

"Now I get it," Willow said, turning from them, but only after sizing up Brett. "You're her girl."

Allie didn't fit in with those girls, either. They looked down at her. They didn't get butch-femme and couldn't understand why Allie sometimes . . .

She liked being a girl. And she liked getting pretty for *her* girl. Her butch. Her Brett.

Those *womyn*, or *wimmin*, would argue any small point of anything and wouldn't understand how to get things done. They'd spend their time fighting over whatever power they could get their hands on, and instead of the oppression bringing them together, it forced them apart.

Allie had seen it before. She preferred doing things and getting things done. Like now. They were working on Rowan's case. Allie was sure they'd find Rowan and figure all this out, discover who was guilty, and send him or her to prison for a good long time. She just knew it.

Allie went into the living room and turned on the TV, low. She didn't want to disturb Brett, Madeline, or Leisa.

It was Allie who had first seduced Brett, but only when she realized Brett was afraid of touching her because she was so young, just seventeen at the time. But she had wanted Brett then, just as she did now. There was something primal about Brett Higgins, something that intrigued, scared, compelled, and drew Allie in.

And Brett knew her just as well, knew what would please her and make her happy, both in and out of bed. Even though she didn't always do it, she knew what to do. Brett was her own woman, and always would be, and that was one of the things that both repelled and drew Allie.

Allie just had to believe that she and Brett had the strength to make it through whatever came their way.

Chapter Six

Friday, 10:37 a.m.

"Brett, I got somebody you wanna meet," Frankie said. "Artie, this here's Brett Higgins."

The man with Frankie was a bit chubby, his belly hanging over his belt. The top of his balding head just about reached Frankie's neck, and he was wearing wrinkled black slacks, a gray blazer, white shirt, and a rather bland, dark tie that was loosened around his neck. There was a slight bulge under his left armpit—not very much firepower. Cop.

"You from Ferndale?" Brett asked with a slight nod of her head.

"Yeah," he said, entering the office and looking around, every bit the detective. "I hear ya got some questions about something."

Brett walked around the desk, sitting on the edge and unconsciously running her fingers along the crease of her pants. Her jacket was on the back of her chair, and her shirtsleeves were rolled up to her elbows, exposing her muscular forearms. Frankie was leaning in the doorframe with his arms crossed in front of his thick chest.

"Rumor has it you guys recently tried to arrest a Detroit cop up there—for murder, in fact."

"Yeah," Artie said. "You got it right." He looked around the office, touching things, running his finger along a shelf and then picking up a photo of Brett with Allie. "You know her?"

"She's my girlfriend."

"Izzat so?" he said, studying Allie's face more closely. "You got good taste, she's pretty hot. I . . ." He trailed off and stopped himself. He put the picture back on the shelf. "What do you want to know?"

Brett thought he was sizing her up, and she didn't like it. "Was there anything unusual about the crime scene?"

"It doesn't matter how many homicides you see, they never become usual—and it's not like we got a lot of murders in Ferndale. But no, in the way you mean, there wasn't. Two bullets went through her, one was left in her, and another went into the wall. A few things were outta place, but there weren't any signs of a forced entry, so it really didn't look like a robbery."

"Any vandalism?"

He grinned at this. "No, nothing. And believe you me, in Ferndale, we take that shit seriously, but there wasn't a single trace or hint that this coulda been a hate crime."

"Are you sure about that?"

"Yeah. As soon as we realized she was a dyke, we looked into that real carefully. After all, a few businesses on Nine Mile have received some threatening notes lately—you might've read about it in *Between the Lines*," he said, referring to the local LesBiGay newspaper. "We don't need no queer-killing spree going on in our town."

Brett ignored his queer-baiting. She wondered why he was doing it, but she wanted something from him, so she played nice. "Why did you go after Rowan, then?"

"There wasn't enough to peg it on those hate-mongers, so we talked with the deceased's brother, Dave St. Claire and his girlfriend, Diane, for a bit and they mentioned something that happened at the bar the night before. The Rainbow Room. You might know it. Anyway, since Abernathy—Rowan—is a cop, it seemed like another dead end. But the folks over at the bar verified she pulled a gun, but somebody took it before she could use it." Artie stopped to look Brett up and down. "Somebody big, tall, all in black, and *butch*. Said whoever it was knew how to handle herself."

"I didn't think she should have a gun in that condition," Brett said, leaning into him.

"We knew the cause of death, and identified the bullets in St. Claire and in the wall. When we saw they matched the gun Rowan had . . . well. Her off-duty gun's a Beretta twenty-five and that was what killed St. Claire . . ." He shrugged his big shoulders, letting her do the math.

"So, okay, fine. You brought her in to be on the safe side. Did she have an alibi?"

"Rowan's *girlfriend* said they got home, went to bed, and stayed there . . ." He let the sentence trail off.

Brett silently assessed him. It was difficult to believe the cops could see past homophobia and be open-minded, especially a cop who looked so much the old-time stereotype Artie did. But she knew, especially along the Woodward Corridor, the cops were getting things like sensitivity training courses—but, really, how often did they actually work? On the other hand, this was Dykedale, where she had walked into the local Blockbuster, which had an "Alternative Lifestyle" section, rented *Birdcage*, *Priscilla*, and *Torch Song Trilogy* and not gotten a raised eyebrow until the fourth movie, which was *Ballroom Dancing For Beginners*. She and Allie had wanted to work on some of their dance moves. Even at that video, the clerk seemed more tickled that a big, bad ass butch like Brett was renting a video like that than anything else.

"Listen, I'd like to help ya, but it looks like she *did* do it. The evidence is stacked against her, and there ain't another explanation in sight. And lemme tell you, her taking off like that isn't really putting any points on her side, if y'know what I mean."

"But she said she was innocent, right?"

"Yeah, she did—right before she took off."

"I've heard that her getting outta there mighta been some sorta inside job?"

Artie barely flinched. "Yup, gotta be. On the one hand, I can't blame her for taking off—the cons inside really don't care too much for cops, but as I said . . ." He shrugged.

Brett nodded. "It makes it look even worse for her. But from what you've said, she didn't have a leg to stand on anyway."

"Yup, that's right."

Brett could tell he was a detective by the way he was still looking around her office, picking things up and inspecting them. Normally this would piss her off, but he *was* helping her, after all. He looked at Allie's picture one more time. "Abernathy had a pic of this woman in her living room. Why?" He looked at Brett.

"Allie used to be a cop. She and Abernathy were partners years ago," Brett said.

"That's why Brett here's looking for info," Frankie said. He stood in the doorway with his arms crossed in front of his massive chest.

Artie looked at the two of them and apparently came to a decision. "She—Abernathy—said her girlfriend wanted to talk to St. Claire. Was convinced she could somehow finally convince the woman to lay off her. Well, St. Claire ended up attacking Abernathy with a fireplace poker, or so Abernathy says. Abernathy pulled her gun. That seemed to put St. Claire back in her place, 'cept that she took one final swipe at Abernathy, hitting her hand and causing the gun to go off. Once." He looked at Brett, his face nearly a blank.

Brett realized he wanted to believe the story. "So how did you get her out of there, Artie?"

He blinked at this one. "Hey, I got a wife and three kids to support, ya think I'd risk my job helping a suspect get away? Even if I don't think she did it?"

"Why? Why don't you think she did it?"

Artie leaned his husky frame in close to her, then half-whispered in a confidential tone, "Too pat. A good cop wouldn't just fly off the handle like that and kill somebody. She woulda planned it out more if she wanted to off the bitch. There wouldn't be such a clear-cut path leading right to her. Too obvious. She wouldn't have used her own gun, and it woulda been easy enough for her to get the damned gunpowder off her hands if she really wanted to. If she'd done it, she woulda cleaned herself up better." He was rambling and apparently knew it. "Look, the reason I'm here is that I know you types can keep your mouths shut, and my gut's telling me she didn't do it, and you might be the chance she's got. The only real chance—y'know what I mean?"

Brett looked at him and nodded. Sometimes you had to work around the rules to get things done.

"We got enough cops these days going bad that we don't need good cops being called bad. That's the real reason I'm so interested in this . . . not that I'm a dyke lover or nothing."

"No, we wouldn't want anyone thinking that. So what? You're hoping that with me being a dyke and all I might be able to find out something you can't?"

Artie grinned. "Oh, I wouldn't go bringing in outsiders. But I also don't look the other way if somebody maybe sends some information my way."

He came to her because he knew she was a lesbian and a criminal. Ironically, in this situation, that meant he could trust her. Knowing she was involved with Allie—an ex-cop and Rowan's old partner—gave him even more reasons. "Lemme know if anything else comes up, 'kay?" Brett said. She stood and walked toward him and pulled some bills, which were money-clipped together, from her pocket. "Well, shit, looks like the smallest thing I got is this," she handed him a hundred. Actually, it was two hundred-dollar bills. They were new, so they stuck together, but she knew it, and he would know it as well. "For gas," she said.

He smiled and took the money, "Yeah, for gas." He turned to Frankie on his way out. "Heya, Frankie, just let me know when ya got another friend with questions, huh?"

"Nice friends ya got there," Brett told Frankie when she heard Artie leave, closing the door behind him.

"Yeah, there's a buncha folks I keep in touch with when I need a hand or a bit of info. But it's not enough to keep 'em on payroll."

"You like those family men, dontcha?"

Frankie let out a grin that was part smirk and part mischief. "I didn't know he was. Course, it's not like I go out drinking with the asshole. Sometimes I just need information. So whatcha gonna do tonight?"

"Dunno. Probably hit the streets—see if I can get any good dope on any of 'em—Rowan, her girl, or Jill. But I still ain't giving up that it mighta been some homophobes."

"So one of the things you got to find is if Jill was still alive when Rowan and Lauren left."

"Yup. But at that time, what'd be the chances anyone'd be calling Jill or that any of the neighbors saw anything?"

"Well, while you decide what to do next, how 'bouts we hit a bar for lunch, maybe you can teach me something 'bout women," Frankie said. He'd often joked he'd had to bring Brett back into the business because he didn't know jack about hiring dancers. And, of course, now he was clueless about the women in the other enterprises Brett had started. He wouldn't know how to hire hot women for pornos, Net stuff, or anything else for that matter.

"Yeah. Works for me. Just gimme a second to call Allie about Artie. Catch her up on it all."

While Brett and Frankie were walking out of the box office, one of the dancers, Hope, was leaving the theater, and another who used the name Precious was going in. Hope was almost Brett's height, with long blond hair, a slender waist, pretty nice tits and long, long legs. Precious was stacked chocolate, with black hair, soft curves, and big tits. Between the two of them, a dyke could be in fucking heaven.

"Maybe we should start calling your honky ass Lazarus," Precious said, wrapping her arms around Brett's neck, pressing those big boobs against her. "Coming back from the dead an' all." Precious was brought up on going to a screamin' Jesus evangelical church every Sunday for sixteen years.

Brett wrapped her arms around Precious, reaching down to grab a handful of that shapely ass. "I take it you girls been talking 'bout me again, eh?"

"I like a woman who can pull that sort of shit off. Comin' outta the grave and all just gots spunk to it, y'know what I mean?"

"But did it take you four years to come up with that line? I been back a while, darlin'."

"We was just telling the new girl about the boss. Including that we might as well call ya Teflon since nothing sticks to you."

Hope, just coming off stage, leaned against the wall, her arms at her sides, naked as the day she was born except for two-inch stiletto heels. "So you're the legendary Brett Higgins."

Brett released Precious, patting her ass. "Get to work and make me some money." Precious went into the theater and Brett turned to assess Hope. The girl couldn't hold a candle to Allie and not just in the looks department. Allie had a sense of class, self-confidence, and humor Hope could never dream of achieving.

"They didn't lie," Hope said, laying her best seductive look on Brett as she eased her eyes up her long, muscular frame.

Brett pulled out her switchblade and used it to clean her fingernails. In one step, she crossed the distance between herself and Hope, flicking the blade so its steel edge glinted in the cheap, fluorescent lighting. She ran the flat of the blade down Hope's breast, her thumb shooting out to tweak the nipple en route. Hope's face had gone as pale as Frankie's white shirt. "It depends on what they told you 'bout me," Brett said with her best snarl, planting her thigh between Hope's legs and pushing them even further apart. "If they called me the dyke-bitch from hell, then I guess they'd be right." She put the blade away. "And if they told you I have an evil sense of humor and love scaring the shit outta you young'uns, they still wouldn't be far off the mark." She winked at Hope, turned, and left.

As soon as Brett and Frankie really thought about it, they realized there weren't exactly a plethora of places where they could eat and view some of the local talent. They decided to postpone their talent search and just have a good lunch at Brett's favorite Italian restaurant, La Dolcé Vita, which was practically next door to their LesBiGay book and gift store, The House of Kinsey.

Brett thought the food at La Dolcé was an improvement over the last restaurant that was located there, Saluté, and the staff was quite friendly as well. She was glad they had a number of waitresses instead of just waiters and even gladder all of those women were quite attractive.

After lunch, Brett went to The House of Kinsey while Frankie went back to the theater. Brett wanted to say hello to Michelle, the manager there. She'd been the manager for quite a few years, in fact. Brett walked in and spotted her immediately. She was still quite the hottie—figure still as trim, long dark hair still as silky as Brett remembered. Michelle was helping a customer at one of the sets of bookshelves Brett herself built several years ago. Brett had started in this business, managing this same bookstore.

Brett had a few at lunch and was in a teasing mood. She silently padded up behind Michelle and laid her hands on Michelle's hips.

"Oh!" Michelle said, spinning around to face Brett and bringing her hands up. When she realized it was Brett, she quickly wrapped them around her neck, pushing herself up against her—stomach against stomach, thigh against thigh, breasts against breasts. "Wow! Long time, no see!"

Brett gasped, amazed at how soft Michelle's body felt, amazed at her good, clean scent. She wrapped her arms around Michelle instinctively, briefly lifting her up off the floor. "Ya know, I'm technically your boss, so we probably shouldn't be doing this."

"Oh, as if the girls over at the theater don't hug you . . . among other things."

"So ya want me to treat you like one of them? Maybe you want to be one of them?"

Michelle pulled away slightly, leaving her hands on Brett's shoulders.

Brett gazed down at her, remembering how they flirted when she was single. Then she remembered the customer Michelle had been helping. She glanced up at her.

"Oh, Brett, I'm sorry this is . . . this is . . ." Michelle fell off in her introduction of the customer, obviously never having gotten her name.

Brett looked over the woman's long red hair and her nice ass and hips. "We've already met."

Tina O'Rourke brazenly looked her up and down, "Brett Higgins. I wish I could say it's been too long—"

"Tina O'Rourke, is there something you ain't been telling me?" Brett replied, glancing around to indicate that Tina was in a queer store. Tina merely raised her eyebrows in response. Brett moved over to her, keeping one hand on Michelle's hip while placing the other on Tina's. Tina didn't move away. "Just know I'm extremely protective of Michelle here. I don't like her hanging around with slime like the O'Rourkes."

Tina didn't fail Brett. No witty repartee from her. She just glared and left.

Brett stayed and chatted with Michelle for a half-hour or so, then left herself. She had been too occupied with Tina's appearance that she didn't bother flirting much more with the cute bookstore manager.

Tina never boded well.

Allie had spent all day learning what she could. She'd been calling all her old friends on the force, trying to find out if anybody knew anything.

Ski and Randi were both in D.C., stuck at a conference of some sort. They were the two people Allie could most rely upon for inside info these days.

Allie hated this. Deep inside, she was a cop, a detective, and she had to rely on Brett, a criminal, for information. Bureaucracy had locked her out and kept her from what she needed to know.

As she called, she made lists—folks she should call to see if they knew anything, people who might be able to get her inside the situation, and those involved with it all.

Everyone was evasive on the phones. Still, this was the initial work needed for such a situation—Googling the players in the case, looking for other background info, tracking each lead online.

She knew she should pound the pavement, but her involvement wasn't official. She first needed to find whatever she could on these people she didn't know much about, and she would follow whatever leads she uncovered. It was the grunt work.

And of course, she kept Brett in the loop via e-mail. Allie didn't have much, but it was better than nothing.

Chapter Seven

Friday, 10:06 p.m.

That night, Brett went ahead with her plans—she had few options. The best nights to work the local bars were Friday and Saturday, so she only had two nights to get information.

If Jill was single, she'd likely hang at the bars. Judging by the display the other night, she liked her booze. Although there were dozens of gay bars in the area, there were only a few at which a woman might hang. Brett reckoned she could find out a lot about Jill at the bars.

Backstreet was only cool on Wednesdays and Saturdays, and even then it was a pretty mixed crowd of boys and girls, most of whom were of the younger set. Sugarbaker's was a sports bar that attracted an older group of women, and Cruisin' Again, or Silent Legacy, which was another bar that somehow had two names, sometimes three, was closer to the airport and was known by some to be a diaper bar, attracting a younger clientele than either Sugarbaker's or The Rainbow Room, the other women's bar.

The Rainbow Room and Sugarbaker's were on Eight Mile, a few miles east of Woodward. If Jill was much of a drinker, those would be the bars she'd frequent because the drive home wouldn't be too bad, whereas Silent Legacy was a half-hour to forty-five minutes away. Brett would check that one last.

She started early at Sugarbaker's, asked a few questions, then headed over to the Rainbow Room, her old hangout when it was still the Railroad Crossing. Ownership had changed, and now there were a few more men, but it was still primarily a women's bar.

At Sugarbaker's, no one recognized Jill's name or photo, which Allie had obtained from Lauren and given to Brett. The early hour didn't put Brett off. She stayed for a beer and shot a game of pool. Sugarbaker's had been around for a dozen years already, and Brett sometimes liked to stop by for a few games and a conversation.

Just before eleven, she left and headed down the street to the Rainbow Room. She was surprised that it was already so busy she had to park in the lot next door.

She paid her cover and headed to the bar for a beer. The same cutie from the other night was tending bar. Brett winked at her and left a ten-dollar tip for her three-dollar drink. Both the bartenders and waitstaff of any place she frequented went out of their way to make sure she got served. She liked it that way, and she did what she could to make sure it stayed that way.

Brett laid the picture down. "Do you know this woman?"

"Yeah, she comes in here all the time." The bartender picked up the ten. "But doesn't tip quite as good as you."

"So she's a regular?"

"Yeah, just about everybody knows Jill." She practically had to yell to be heard over the loud dance music.

"Is there anything else you can tell me about her?"

"She has a bit of a temper. Likes to start fights, get into 'em. Seems to have a lot of cash."

"Anyone in particular she hangs with?"

She shrugged. "Comes in here with a lot of different women. Always here when we've got dancers. That's about all I can think of."

"Thanks for your help," Brett said with a wink. She quickly made a tour of the bar, checking out the dance floor, the patio, the side area, and walking around all three sides of the dance floor. Brett almost regretted having worn jeans and a black leather vest instead of shorts. Of course, she didn't really wear shorts. Allie got her to occasionally wear them when they lived in California while they were on the lam.

She recognized some faces in the crowd of women. Some had been regulars when she was, and she wondered if like herself, they were just here for the night or if they were still regulars, jumping from bed to bed, love to love in search of something too perfect for this world or something that would ease whatever hell they were in.

A voice came over the loudspeakers, temporarily drowning out the backbeat that took over her body and pulsed through her like her blood, announcing that the show would start in just a few minutes.

Brett looked over the room, trying to see if anyone from the other night was there, but the faces were mostly unfamiliar. But she approached the few people she recognized with the photos, asking if they knew anything.

She was just playing a losing hand, as it turned out. Everyone clammed up on her. But then the music changed. Brett thought about taking off since she really didn't have much of an interest in the show here, but the first dancer came out and made eye contact.

The girl's name was Amber. She had long, red hair and a shapely yet slender frame. Brett smiled. She pushed to the front of the crowd and made a show of pulling a fifty from her wallet. She held it between her index and middle fingers and waved it about slightly until the redhead noticed her.

Amber danced up to her, slowly drawing her onto the dance

floor. Brett tucked the bill into the waist of her tight black jeans. Amber slowly fell to her knees, drawing the bill out with her teeth. She took it from her mouth and put it back in Brett's hand, which she then guided to the elastic of her thong. She danced next to Brett, pushing her body against Brett's. The crowd hollered, laughing their encouragement.

"I need help with something," Brett said.

Amber wrapped her arms around Brett's neck, pulling her in for a long, slow one. Brett caressed her ass as they kissed.

When they parted, Amber said, "Ask whatever it is later, backstage," and then danced off for more tip money.

Brett went back to the bar and waited until both Amber and another dancer named Erika were done with their acts. She'd seen Amber whisper to Erika as they passed each other—Amber leaving the spotlight, Erika entering it. Brett knew what Amber had said—she'd told Erika about Brett.

When Erika left the dance floor at the end of her number, Brett walked up behind her and placed a hand on her hip.

"She's with me," Erika said to the dude running the spotlight who was about to try to stop Brett. She didn't even need to look at Brett—she'd just taken her hand and led her to the space she shared with Amber backstage.

"You're still not here for a happy, are you?" Amber said. She was leaning back against the sink in this now unused bathroom, waiting for Brett and looking right at her.

"No, not right now," Brett said. "But you should watch what you say to me. Your dreams really might come true some day."

"It's not me who likes you," Amber said. "It's Erika."

They were in the bathroom, near the stall. Apparently Erika and Amber had again staked it out as their own territory in the jumbled confusion of people getting dressed and changing costumes for the show. Brett was pretty sure this was exactly the same place she'd last talked with the two girls a while ago when she was investigating the serial killing of local erotic dancers.

"So what do you want this time?" Erika said.

"Information," she pulled Jill's picture from her back pocket.

"Uh-huh, sure," Erika said, taking the picture with a suggestive smile. "You've got more pictures than anyone I know." Last time, Brett had shown them pictures as well.

"Do you know her?" Brett asked.

Erika glanced at the photo and laughed. "Yeah, I know Jill." She leaned around Brett to look at Amber. "Didja catch that? She wants to know about Jill."

She heard Amber's deep, rich laugh behind her. "Yeah, it figures. Oh, dear God, please tell me big bad butch does *not* have *sleazy* pictures of *Jill*!"

"No. It's just a regular pic," Erika said.

"Thank God!"

Brett pocketed the photo and leaned back against the wall. "Is there anything you two care to share?"

Erika shrugged. "She was always good for a coupla drinks, long as you didn't take her too seriously. Coupla my friends were all set to pack up and move in with her when she dumped 'em flat on their faces." Erika's eyes were open and teasing, she didn't look much like a lover-done-me-wrong sort.

"Drinks was all?"

"Drinks was all," Amber said. "Neither of us cares much for anything stronger."

In fact, if Brett's senses weren't lying, neither of these women had even had a drink so far that night. They both sounded and acted stone-cold sober, and there wasn't a hint of a smell of alcohol about them. She didn't know these two very well, but she'd never seen them drunk or high or anything so far, so she had no reason to question that. "But did Jill?"

"I think she toys with some other shit," Erika said. "She offered me some coke once, and I passed. Sometimes she's kinda outta it, like she's been doing something, but with the way she drinks, it's hard to tell."

"*Did* Jill?" Amber suddenly said. She had been staring at Brett for a few moments. When Brett didn't reply, she walked over to her, again appraising her. "You said, 'did Jill,' not 'does Jill.'"

"And your point is?" Brett finally replied when Amber was standing directly in front of her.

"Why did you say *did*?"

Brett stood from her leaning position and, with gazes locked, she approached Amber, who, with each of Brett's forward steps, took a step back, until she was against the wall. "Jill's dead," Brett finally whispered. "And a friend asked me to look into her death. So that's what I'm doing."

"Who's your friend?" Erika asked.

Brett slowly pulled away from Amber and faced Erika. "Rowan Abernathy."

"Rowan?" Amber asked. "As in Lauren and Rowan?"

"You know her?"

"Hell, yes. They come here a bit, too. I can't see what Lauren ever saw in Jill in the first place, but I can tell you Jill was outta her mind thinking she'd ever get Lauren back from Rowan."

"Doesn't sound like you'll really miss Jill," Brett said, looking at Amber, but glancing over at Erika.

"Nobody 'round here will," Erika said. "As I said, she was good for free drinks, maybe a place to crash. Women used her and she used them—pictured herself a female Casanova or something."

"So did you ever go home with her, Erika?" Brett asked.

Erika glanced at Amber, then back at Brett. "Yeah, once, about a year or so ago. I had a few too many to drink and hadn't been coming here very much, so I didn't really know her. She looked like a decent catch. She was decent looking, obviously had money. Shit. So I went for it." She winked at Brett. "At least she was a decent lay."

"Sounds like you're real broken up about it." Brett was sure they were hiding something, but she couldn't figure out what.

"I'm sure she's played some people real wrong—I mean, occasionally I've seen her get hit with something or had a drink thrown at her, but it's not like after one night I was ready to marry her or anything. Hell, even last weekend when she was in here we were flirting and shit—she was still good for a free drink or two . . ."

The thought that had been scratching at Brett's brain suddenly came to the forefront. "So there might be women who were pissed off enough at her to take her out?"

"Hell," Amber said, "you see the headlines—people are willing to kill over much smaller things. Doesn't take much imagination to figure out somebody'd be willing to kill over something like that." Erika nodded her agreement. "The entire 'if I can't have her, nobody else will,' routine, you know."

"Did you ever sleep with her?" Brett asked Amber.

"No, I didn't. She's not my type."

Brett pulled a business card from her pocket and handed it to Erika. "Well, if you think of anything, give me a call."

Erika took the card, which stated simply, "Paradise Enterprises, Brett Higgins, Manager," lightly brushing her fingers against Brett's. "I still have the last one you gave me. You never gave me a call, though."

"Oh. Well, I kinda figured things out that last time. Caught the killer and all. Didn't need anything else."

"You sure you just manage some sleaze joints," Amber said. " 'Cause it's really sounding more and more like you're a cop or detective or something."

Brett smiled at her. "Yeah, hon, I'm sure. I'm just checking up on this for a friend."

"A friend, huh?" Erika said. She wrapped her arms around Brett's shoulders. "A *friend* friend, or a special friend, or . . . ?"

"You seem more like somebody who'd have business associates and acquaintances. Girlfriends. Exes." Amber said. "Not really one for *friends*, though."

"I have friends," Brett said. "And sometimes they ask me for help. So I help 'em. This is one of those times."

"Why are your friends so interested in all of this?" Amber asked, arms crossed in front of her.

Brett shrugged. "The woman who looks to be going down for this is an old partner of a good friend of mine. We'd like to find out who did it."

"You know," Erika said, "we never did get that drink last time. Why don't you hang around, and we can talk after the next set?"

Brett smiled at her. "I'll see. I need to ask around a bit more anyway."

"Gee, way to make a girl feel important," Erika said.

"Sorry. I guess I got a bit of foot-in-mouth going on tonight," Brett said. "Listen, maybe I might see ya after the next set." She smiled at them and bowed out.

She was just a few feet away when she heard Amber say to Erika, "Why didn't you tell her about Jill?"

"Let's just not talk about it," Erika said.

"But—"

"No. Really. I don't want to talk about it, okay?"

"Okay, fine. Whatever."

Then Amber and Erika stopped talking.

Brett spent the next hour cruising the bar, asking more questions. Jill, Rowan, and Lauren were pretty well known in the community as it turned out. Apparently, from what she heard, there had been a great many other scenes like the one she had witnessed a few nights before.

For the most part, no one seemed real sorry to hear of Jill's untimely demise and of the handful who already knew about it, at least half were glad Rowan finally gave her what was coming to her. It seemed as if Rowan and Lauren were pretty well liked, whereas Jill wasn't. What intrigued Brett was that usually a couple didn't gain such open admiration and respect as Rowan and Lauren had amongst the bar set. The other thing that piqued her interest was that several people mentioned Jill's money, so she seemed to have quite a bit of it, but no one really knew from where, although several people grudgingly admitted she was a decent artist.

Brett flirted with both Erika and Amber and tipped them when they danced again. She fooled around with them on the dance floor while the crowd hooted and hollered their appreciation. She still wasn't sure if she was going to hang around to have a drink with them, though. What finally won out was that she wanted to find out what they had been discussing just after she'd left their changing area.

Brett was sitting and sipping her beer after the show, waiting for the two dancers to join her. When they finally sat down across from her, they were both in sundresses and sandals, long hair floating about their faces that were scrubbed clean of all the heavy makeup they'd been wearing earlier.

After her many years of dealing with strippers and dancers, Brett really preferred these two like this—natural.

"I really have to wonder if you two do everything together," Brett asked, letting her gaze trail over the two quite beautiful women. She signaled for the waitress. "What's your poison?"

"Corona with a lime," Amber said.

"Screaming Orgasm, please," Erika said, looking right at Brett. "Bet you're really good with those."

Brett spent the next hour dancing with the two cuties, sometimes as a group, sometimes it was just her and Erika, once with Amber.

But still, she hadn't gotten a further clue about what the two had been talking about after she left their dressing area.

Chapter Eight

Saturday, 12:37 a.m.

Brett quickly glanced behind her as she jumped into her black Jimmy. No one was following. She pulled onto Eight Mile and did a Michigan left, wherein one has to first turn right in order to turn left to head east and back toward home. She flipped through the radio stations before finally pushing in a CD of Melissa Etheridge, trying to focus on the case to get her mind off Amber and Erika with their enticing eyes, sexy voices, and seductive bodies.

She wondered why Allie hadn't explained about Jill and her thick wallet. Lots of questions, no answers. What was up with Jill and Lauren? How had Lauren ended up with Rowan? After all, from talking around the bar, it seemed as if Jill wasn't letting go too easily. It was annoying as hell when folks deliberately kept information from her.

She turned right on Woodward, planning on following that to

Main Street in Royal Oak. She and Allie actually lived just a few minutes away from the bar and could take either the expressway or the surface streets home.

Beyond all the unanswered questions, there were too damned many loose ends in the mess. For all she knew, the perp could be whoever was sending threatening notes to queer-owned businesses in Ferndale.

Brett realized she was in Ferndale. She went past Nine Mile and did yet another Michigan left—the damned things were all over the place. She never could figure out why they didn't just put in left-turn lanes. She drove down Nine Mile. Ferndale was a pretty homey community and even along this short stretch of Nine, she easily found three full-size rainbow flags flying from different establishments. No wonder it was often called "Dykedale."

She had read the newspaper accounts about the threatening notes. They reported that the police thought it might be high school students, which meant they wouldn't be very likely to actually carry through on their threats. Not suburban high schoolers in this part of town, anyway.

She stopped herself and thought, okay, anything was possible, but if whoever killed Jill was the same person who'd been leaving the threatening notes, they probably would have also left some sort of a sign at the scene of the murder because what good would it be to off someone for being gay unless you let people know that's why they died? Unless it started off with them only threatening Jill and things got out of hand. They hadn't planned on actually killing her, they just wanted to harass her, and she was killed by *accident*.

If her death had been an accident, they really wouldn't want to sign it. The murder. That's why they didn't leave any signs that it was a murder about homophobia.

But on the other hand, there seemed to be a lot of women pissed off at Jill. And all it took was one to commit murder. Brett could almost see it: Once upon a time Jill picks up some woman at the bar, takes her home with her, and the next morning the woman is all ready to rent a U-Haul and Jill says, "Yeah, I got your number, and maybe I'll catch ya Friday at the bar." The woman goes home heartbroken—one of a million or so women Jill'd done this to along the way. But this particular woman is out drinking on Wednesday and sees Jill hitting on Lauren at the bar. The woman has a few more, then goes to Jill's home, which she's driven by a few hundred or thousand times since that night, to talk to Jill, just talk to her. Jill, already knowing the woman, would let her in, would talk with her. And the woman would leave without bothering to make it look like burglary because she was scared, scared that she had acted so brutally. She would've run scared as soon as she realized what she'd done, that she had let her anger get so out of control.

But what was the chance she would've had the same type of gun Rowan did? And did Jill have a gun? Could this woman have used Jill's own gun against her?

Again, Brett thought, too many questions, not enough answers.

But Brett knew there had to be a reason the killer hadn't tried to cover his or her steps better. Or maybe framing Rowan was the cover, and that was the reason it hadn't been made to look like a burglary.

Brett pulled into the lot across the street from Affirmations and A Woman's Prerogative, the local lesbian bookstore. Back in the old days, when she used to go to the occasional women's rap group at Affirmations, she'd park in this lot. But this time, instead of checking herself out in the mirror and maybe spritzing on some cologne and locking a briefcase filled with cash in the trunk, she pulled her briefcase out of the backseat and looked at the notes she had taken while discussing the case with Allie.

She quickly found what she was looking for—Jill's address. Allie and Randi hadn't been able to get in to investigate the crime scene, but Allie'd given Brett the address. Probably hoping she'd behave as she usually did, which is to say, not at all. In the middle of the night, Brett didn't really see why she'd need permission.

While she was at it, she also pulled out her .357, a flashlight, and her lock picks, tools of the trade for tracking down dancers who were late for shows. Sometimes these women were doped up, but sometimes they had gone somewhere after a show with a trick, and it was a lot cheaper to open up the motel door than to smash it in when the men they were with tried to tie them up, kidnap them, or worse.

Brett figured she'd always been lucky that a john was only occasionally armed—they usually just had to overpower the women and tie them up. Of course, Brett had always been armed, but it was a lot less messy if they weren't.

At one point, Brett had considered issuing a memo to the dancers stating that management preferred it if they did their johns out back in their cars. It'd have been a lot easier tracking their asses down that way. You'd think the dancers would've figured out that the less money the boys spent on rooms, the more they could spend on getting laid.

That was the past, and now she just wanted to take a simple look around Jill's house. Before she started the car, she again looked across the street, wondering about the threatening notes being left at the queer establishments around town. She climbed out of her car and walked around the groups of buildings, casing them. When she didn't see anything suspicious, she lit a cigarette and hung out on the half wall between the lesbian bookstore and the LesBiGay community center, but no one was around. Things seemed quiet even at the Irish Pub across the street from the place. Brett went back to her car.

She easily found Jill's house. She knew she had been here before, the neighborhood was very familiar. She drove by Jill's house, then around the neighboring blocks. Down the road a bit some people were throwing a party, and cars were parked all along the street in both directions. Brett added her Jimmy to the rows of vehicles, grabbed her gear, looked around for any witnesses and slipped out into the night.

While she drove around the blocks, Brett noticed that the house that backed up to Jill's was dark. It looked like the owners were out for the night—maybe at the neighbor's party. She cut through their backyard and hopped the fence into Jill's yard.

The grass was thick and quickly becoming overgrown with the recent rain. Brett crossed the yard in a few broad strides, but changed direction en route, suddenly realizing that some improvements had been made to the older home.

Most of the homes in Royal Oak and Ferndale were at least fifty years old and Brett knew from old friends and looking at homes in the area that many had somewhat similar layouts.

Jill's house was a two-story structure rather than the single-level bungalows so popular in the area, and it had been extended in the back with an addition, a patio, and French doors.

Curtains were drawn over the back doors. Brett figured there'd be a side door with an old lock, whereas these doors might have a slightly more complicated, newer lock. She moved along the side of the house to the side door and pulled out her picks.

Picking a lock was rather like playing a musical instrument—or a woman. Slowly entering, feeling for just the right spots and then caressing the tumblers. It wasn't something you did brutally, but with feeling, using your hands to gently stroke the tumblers until they gave you what you wanted.

Brett Higgins liked using her hands to get what she wanted.

The lock gave, and she turned it with the tension bar until she was able to quietly step into the house. There weren't any cars outside nor any lights on inside. She had every reason to believe the house was deserted—only thing left was the reading of the will and the property disposed of. Still, she didn't want to attract any undue attention from the neighbors—she was quiet and didn't turn on any lights.

She flipped on the flashlight. Steps in front of her led down to the basement. She climbed down, smelling a vague mustiness as she descended. Brett guessed the back room had been a recent addition to the home—the basement didn't seem as big as the main floor. Although she didn't see any water stains or puddling, she had a feeling it had only recently been waterproofed because of the smell that clung to the walls and floor.

The basement was simple and apparently used for storage. One corner just to the side of the staircase held the laundry area, complete with folding table, machine, dryer, and tubs. On the other side of the staircase was a work area with a bench, several toolboxes, and racks of wrenches hanging on the walls. The far corner of the basement, which Brett imagined was just under the front room, held a wall of boxes, and the rest of the basement had shelves crammed with various other things from gardening tools to house paint and a car buffer.

Brett spent a few moments opening the most easily accessible boxes and studying the way they were stacked. It appeared they had not been recently disturbed because a thin layer of dust covered them. It didn't take very long to realize why they had not been disturbed—the top few boxes contained a fake Christmas tree with tacky white flocking, a bunch of men's suits, ties, and shirts, and some other old clothing that looked like it was waiting for someone to remember to take them to the Salvation Army.

Brett closed the boxes and went back upstairs and into the kitchen. It was simple and clean but smelled a bit off. She traced one strange odor to the trash underneath the sink and another to the refrigerator where something that had once resembled a pizza resided. Obviously no one had yet been through the house to claim belongings or clear it out. That was definitely a good thing.

The kitchen, although tastefully done with almost-new appliances and an inlaid parquet floor, wasn't one of the most-used rooms in the house. The lack of real food and spices clued her in, but the oven was far too clean and the stove unsplattered, whereas the top of the fridge was covered with a layer of dust. There was only one pot and one pan in the cupboards.

But as Brett wandered through the first floor with its hardwood floors, expensive Oriental rugs, signed artwork, damask curtains and sofas, she became aware that whoever had decorated it not only had taste but also a lot of money. She ran her hand over the texture of the curtains, briefly sunk into the down-filled cushions on the couch and carefully examined the carved frames on the paintings. She knew how much this shit cost because of her recent shopping escapades with Allie.

In the corner of the front room Brett found a stain on the floor just barely touching the edge of a rug. This was where Jill must have fallen. There were two neat bullet holes in the wall behind where Jill must've been standing and another in the floor. Brett remembered that Jill was shot twice—one was left in her, and another lodged into the wall. So these shots came from different angles.

She saw the fireplace with an expensive stoking set nearby. Someone had apparently replaced the poker that Jill allegedly attacked Rowan with that fateful night.

The stuff in the house screamed money, and Brett found this the only extraordinary thing about the main floor. Allie hadn't mentioned anything about what Jill did for a living or about where she got all her cash. Brett's interest was piqued.

She walked into the back room, playing her light across the large area. She had never paid too much attention to the fine arts, but she figured she could identify a painter's lair when she found one. The place was littered with paints, canvasses, easels. The sheer quantity of work and its priority in setting seemed to indicate that Jill did this professionally. Although Brett had heard that Jill was a painter, she hadn't quite believed it until now. This room had obviously been created just for this.

Brett lifted the edge of a sheet lying over a completed work. She thought it was okay. But could stuff like that pay for a joint like this? Before turning to the staircase, Brett played the flashlight over the room one more time. Something glinted in the light. She walked over to take a closer look and found several pictures of Lauren and Jill together, obviously taken when they were still a couple.

She went up the staircase, hoping to find a more intimate room upstairs, although she vaguely recalled having heard about art as being a portal to the soul or some other nonsense like that. She needed something concrete, something that would point to her murderer, give someone a good enough reason to want Jill dead.

The second floor had a full bath, a bedroom, and something Brett presumed to be a study or office of some sort. The bedroom was dominated by a queen size bed, and an oak bedroom set, complete with a fucking wardrobe. Sheesh, with a setup like this, you'd think she'd live in Bloomfield Hills or Grosse Pointe, not Ferndale. Of course, Brett also could've afforded Bloomfield Hills, but she and Allie chose to live in the friendlier, less austere Royal Oak.

Besides a picture of Lauren on the bedside table, she found nothing of interest in the bedroom, aside from the fact that Jill, with all her tough-guy exterior, owned almost a dozen lacy bras and a drawer full of silky underwear. Brett suppressed a chuckle and made her way to the last room.

Bingo! The room had two windows, one looking out onto the street, the other overlooking the neighbors. A large bookcase, not half-filled, covered one wall, and in one corner of the room was a desk with a computer on it. The room also contained a filing cabinet and a closet with a stack of boxes, the sort used to ship copy paper.

Brett pulled the blinds tight, then turned on the computer. She was thankful, albeit amazed, that it was a PC. She had understood that creative types generally preferred Macs. While the computer booted up, she pulled a photo album off the bookshelf and flipped through it.

Obviously, Jill had still been hung up on Lauren. If Brett hadn't clued in on that earlier, this album was enough to make her do so. Pictures of Lauren, and of Lauren and Jill together, were the theme of this album. Brett thought she recognized the backgrounds in a few of the photos, so she looked more closely, trying to place the type of furnishings and location of buildings in the back half of the album. She stopped at a nighttime picture of Lauren sitting on top of a huge boulder, which was painted white with the big black letters J loves L. Brett studied the tree-lined background, a river glinting in the moonlight through the trees. It was taken at Michigan State University, Brett's alma mater. The two women must've gone to school up there together.

It took her only a few moments to realize the computer was used mostly for purposes of pleasure—there was an Internet hookup and a few basic programs, but nothing that caught her interest. She left it running while she searched the rest of the place.

Jill didn't seem to keep any sort of a diary or journal, though Brett did find an address book that she pocketed.

One entire drawer of the filing cabinet was filled with memorabilia of Jill's relationship with Lauren—more photographs, love letters, even old shopping lists. The woman was obsessed. In another drawer were items also of a rather personal nature, things that weren't filed but kept in shoe boxes and scattered loose throughout the drawer.

Brett ruffled through the papers, looking for anything that caught her attention. It was a rather random method, not at all official or professional, but after all, the only thing she was really professional at was crime.

There were quite a few personal letters written in rather feminine scripts, more than a handful of which were scented with perfume. Brett flipped through them, wondering if she should take them to read later—after all, it might've been a jilted lover that done her wrong.

Or maybe the girlfriend in a torrid love affair?

Anyway, from what she'd heard earlier, she knew not to simply write off such possibilities. One letter grabbed her attention. Brett read it:

Jill,

I can't say I'm surprised. Not really. Because I'm not.

I walked into this knowing who and what you are—good for a few drinks, a couple of laughs, and one helluva time in bed. But now I know the truth, that you're afraid, just like the rest of us. You say Rowan stole

Lauren from you, and that you and Lauren are meant to get back together. You're meant to grow old together, but the truth is it's easier to remain in the past, easier to say it'll happen with her, and you're just waiting for that, biding your time.

You're scared of trusting anybody else, most of all yourself.

An artist needs to have inner turmoil, and the ability to spend lots of time by herself. And you're a damned good artist, and it'll just keep getting better.

What I'm saying is that someday you're gonna need somebody, and need to be able to trust somebody. It'll happen sooner or later, and you might as well get it over with.

Trust me, because, honey, I won't let you fall.

Erika

No, Brett thought to herself, it couldn't be the same Erika. Erika the dancer. Erika the banker. Erika from earlier that night at the bar.

The other three drawers of the cabinet contained file folders filled with more practical documents like old income tax returns, credit card statements, bank notices, and legal contracts.

In just a few minutes Brett realized that Jill did indeed have quite a bit of money and was, for all intents, living on just the interest. She also had her own income as an artist, something she seemed to do with reasonable success if the gallery contracts she had in her files were any indication.

In the kitchen she found a paper bag, which she brought back up to the study to liberate selected items of information from their current environment. The cops had probably already taken anything of interest to them, and if they hadn't—well, then they really weren't working fast enough to be of any good to anyone anyhow.

Chapter Nine

Saturday, 2:30 a.m.

When Brett finally made it home, she was surprised to find Madeline still awake. She was sitting on the couch with her bare feet propped up on the chest in front of it. She was wearing some lightweight kimono-type thing and had a book in her lap.

"Allie's asleep upstairs," Maddy said.

Brett walked into the kitchen where she grabbed a Miller Lite before she sat on the loveseat and lit a smoke.

"Did you meet with any success tonight?" Maddy asked when it became apparent Brett wasn't about to offer anything.

"Nope. Not really. Got a few more suspects and a lot more questions."

"Perhaps discussing it might bring things into the light."

Brett grinned. "You just want to know what I've been up to, nosy."

Madeline met her gaze suddenly, freezing her in place. "I have no question that I will be unable to elicit a full report from you, for there are certain things you keep so deeply within yourself they may never see the light of day. However, with regard to this case, yes, I am curious as to what you have uncovered."

"Jill had money. I want to know where it came from. She was a painter, apparently a fairly successful one at that, but I doubt she could have gotten so much dough from just that." Madeline watched as Brett got up and paced the floor. "This means that whoever inherits would be a likely suspect. I want to know who gets it, where it came from, and just how much there is." Her mind was racing, running up and down the many loopholes throughout the entire case Artie had presented. Maybe it wasn't as open-and-shut against Rowan as Brett had thought.

"Those questions probably will not be that difficult to answer. Most certainly the police will be looking into that as well."

"They probably will, or they'll at least know, so I can find out that way. Hopefully. But there's also the matter of gay businesses in Ferndale being harassed recently with threatening notes and such. I don't think it'd be related to the murder, but there's always the chance. Slim as it may be."

"Did you find out anything else? Like when you were at the bar?"

Brett wondered how Madeline had known what she had said so far hadn't come from the bar, although some parts of it had. She shrugged and said, "Jill was a player. Hurt lots of women, I'm sure, so any one of them coulda done her, too."

"Love, money, and revenge—the classic reasons for murder. Either passion or greed gone awry so that reason no longer matters."

Brett remembered Madeline saying such things just a few years before with regard to a murder she and Allie had witnessed. At that time as well, Madeline had brought up the classic motives for murder.

Brett then thought about Jill's living room, imagining it with her body lying on the floor. She thought backward, running the film in reverse, seeing how Jill might've ended up lying on the floor, how she would've been standing before the shots were fired.

She suddenly wondered how many bullets were missing from Rowan's gun.

Thinking about Jill lying dead made her think about other dead bodies she had seen in the past. There were quite a number from her old life, but there were other deaths that had affected her even before her life of crime.

"Brett? Brett dear?" she suddenly heard Madeline's voice and realized she had been falling off to La La Land.

"Hmmm?" she asked in response.

"Where did you go?"

Brett was laying in the loveseat, her head resting on one arm with her legs tossed over the other. She saw the trees outside dancing in the faint breeze and felt that same breeze gently caress her face. She took a drag on her cigarette and exhaled slowly. When she finally spoke, her voice almost surprised her with its huskiness.

"When I was younger," she said, "I lived in a really bad part of Detroit, so I knew of people who bought it—I mean, some of 'em even got nailed in school. But I really didn't have too many friends, I was kinda a loner." There were so many cracks and crevices in her soul she had never shown to another, just because it didn't fit the entire image she had built for herself. But it had taken quite a bit to become who she was now. She continued.

"When I was fourteen, I started working. By the time I was seventeen, I was managing a fast food joint, a McDonald's, working fifty or so hours a week. I wanted to be able to go to college even if I couldn't get a scholarship. Anyway, it was there that I finally started making a coupla friends."

She remembered Rosalyn's brown eyes, thick black hair, fine features, and skin the color of creamed coffee. And creamed was what happened to Brett every time she looked at the woman.

Although Rosalyn was a year younger, Brett thought of her as older with her full figure compared to Brett's own tall, lanky bone-thinness.

Brett had occasionally glimpsed Rosalyn in the halls of their high school, but never had the courage to speak to her. Then, one day, she came in to the store, and it was Brett who had to train her. By the end of the shift, she knew the world wasn't a fair place, as if she had ever had any questions about it. Not only was Rosalyn gorgeous, she was smart, and nice, and had a sense of humor as well. By the end of Rosalyn's first month at the restaurant, Brett woulda jumped through hoops for her. If Rosalyn ever knew how Brett felt about her, she never let on, but she was the only person Brett let get anywhere near her during those terrible years. After all, Brett's dear cousin had just disappeared from her life for the most part.

Somehow Rosalyn snuck through all of Brett's carefully laid traps and safeguards. She was the only one who could touch Brett without Brett jumping back and trying to protect herself, she was the only one who could hug Brett and make everything all better, and at the time, she was the only person to see Brett cry. Crying was a sign of weakness, defenselessness, need. Although Brett often thought she might've fit those qualifications, she'd never admit that to anyone else in the entire fucking world.

Madeline cleared her throat. Brett looked up at her. "Sometimes, if I wasn't working late at one job or the other, I'd go back to the store to hang out with the crew while they closed." It was her excuse to get out of the house. Sometimes she'd just wander the streets for hours, even though a lone white woman on the streets of Detroit after dark was probably as safe as doing a bungee jump with a cord fifteen feet too long. Or as safe as staying home often was for Brett.

Rosalyn was working that night, so Brett went to the restaurant, just to be near her, hear her laugh. Sometimes just that would make Brett forget about how sore she was where her father rammed her into a wall, or the stench of her brothers' sweat when they came for a nighttime visit. "It was two-thirty in the morning when I walked up to the store. Jeff, the maintenance man, saw me coming and came outside to let me in. I grinned at him, started to say something but he interrupted." She looked outside the window, vividly remembering the warmth of the air, the way the breeze teased through her hair on that night more than a decade ago, a night she could remember like it was yesterday. "He looked at me and said, 'I got some bad news. Paul and Rosalyn were out on a beer run when their car was hit by a drunk driver. I just heard it on my police scanner.' Jeff had some weird predilection toward that damned box, it was ghastly, really, the way he listened to that all the time instead of the radio or TV."

The words were like a death knell. It was as if time stopped, she couldn't really do anything, so she just collapsed against the flagpole. Jeff hadn't said anybody died or anything, but Brett knew that Jeff wouldn't've said it like that if they were all right.

She thought of Paul, trying to distract her mind from its real worries. They always called him The Foreigner, with his dark, Chaldean skin, and the scar on his forehead from his last car accident. He spoke with a slight accent and came into the restaurant when he wasn't working to order "a double-cheeseburger, no onions, extra pickles, and don't fuck it up." Brett had known him for almost two years at that point. He had a silly sort of smile that Brett could clearly picture even now.

Brett sat up on the loveseat. "Donna came out. She said they'd just gotten a hold of the cops, so I went with her to the hospital. She was driving quite fast, and it was real late, so the roads were practically empty. But we saw some flashing lights in front of us and realized they had closed down most of the intersection. I think we both knew at the same time that that was where it had happened. Before Donna could stop the car, I jumped out and ran over to see the car. It was twisted and smashed, with the sides caved in like a fucking pop can.

"I was fucking sick to my stomach. I just had to see it. I ran right through a sprinkler, not really noticing anything. It was like my mind had shut off, and I couldn't really think or feel, I could just look and watch. I stood and stared at that . . . that mangled wreckage and my heart was beating and my . . . my soul was just locked up with my stomach dropping.

"I just had to look at the damned thing to know Rosalyn wasn't alive, even though I tried to tell myself she was. I stared at the car, thinking that we had celebrated her birthday in it, that we had driven all over town in it, and the last time I had seen Rosalyn was in it."

Brett, Paul, Rosalyn, and Steve had driven around in Paul's car, passing beers around while listening to very loud music, occasionally singing aloud to things like Lisa Lisa's hit "Head to Toe." It had been a fun night. Brett would have sworn Rosalyn was flirting with her when she'd look into the backseat at Brett, pass the beer over to her, smile and joke with her.

Brett looked over at Madeline, who sat calmly watching her, just listening. "A cop came up to me, asked if there was a problem. I just wanted to scream at him that of course there was a fucking problem—one of the few people I had ever loved had been in that goddamned car, that car that looked like some sorta broken toy, something ready for the trash heap." Brett downed the rest of her beer as she paced, then lit another cigarette when she went to grab another beer. "Instead, I just ran away. Donna had to race down the street to catch up with me." Brett suddenly realized she was talking almost like she had in those days, with some of the Ebonic twang she had grown up with.

Brett could no longer look at Madeline, even though she knew Madeline was intentionally keeping silent, trying to make Brett forget her presence. A part of her wanted to run and hide, but another part knew she had to tell this story for once and for all. A coldness had settled through her limbs, resting her, giving her the peace the alcohol could not. She looked at Madeline. "We got to the hospital and discovered Paul was there, but not Rosalyn. Paul was in bad shape and couldn't have visitors. Nobody knew shit about Rosalyn though. We, the group of us, went to a coupla different hospitals around the area, but nobody found anything, so's we went to McDonald's, and finally the assistant manager, Colin, decided to call Rosalyn's and Paul's houses. Nobody was at Paul's, or else they were passed out drunk or stoned, in which case nobody was really home."

Brett stood staring out the front window, silently smoking her cigarette and sipping her beer for so long that Madeline finally said, "What about Rosalyn?"

"Colin called her house next. I remember I was standing in the drive-thru area, but I could hear everything. Jeff was standing near Colin, and Donna was over by the front counter with Sue. Colin dialed the number, and Rosalyn's sister Becky picked up on the other end. I just couldn't think about what I was feeling, so instead I thought about how amazing it was anything could've survived the twisted heap that was now Paul's car. Then I heard Colin tell Rosalyn's sister to stop crying. I couldn't help but think that Rosalyn was just a bit younger than me, and I kept remembering all the times I'd been in that car with Paul, or Colin, or Steve or . . . or Rosalyn." Brett whipped around to face Madeline, she knew she wasn't herself, but there wasn't anything she could do. "All the while Colin kept fucking telling Becky to stop crying, and I just couldn't stop shivering." She paced a few steps, ran her hand back through her hair, and looked at Madeline. "Part of me was thinking that I coulda been in that car. If I had been working that night, then I woulda been in that car—I *woulda* gone out with Paul to pick up a case. And it woulda been me, not Rosalyn, who bought it that night."

Some part of Brett heard Madeline ask what had happened to Rosalyn, but all Brett could think of was that wrecked car, and how she had suddenly realized that night that she was only mortal, made of flesh and blood. No one is immune to sadness, to harm, to loss.

"Colin dropped the phone," Brett finally whispered. All these years later she still couldn't say it out loud. She gathered all her courage, all her strength, and said, "Colin dropped the phone, and all I could hear was Steve, Paul, Rosalyn, and me singing 'Head to Toe' inside of my head, and then I heard Colin say, in this dead voice, 'Oh my God.'" Brett turned and looked at Madeline. "No one needed to be told what had happened to Rosalyn."

Brett felt her body rocked by the spasms of pain she had felt that night, the knife-through-her-soul feeling as she realized the only person she had ever loved was dead—dead because of some stupid son of a bitch who ran a red light when he was dead drunk.

Brett Higgins was a woman who had to wait until she was a full five years old before her folks gave her a name, a woman who had survived more than she ever wanted to remember between her father and brothers and a mother who never wanted a daughter, and decided to stop feeling after Rosalyn died. Love became a four-letter word until Storm died, and Brett realized what she had lost in Allie. Rosalyn was an infatuation, a crush, whereas Allie was . . . Allie was perfection, a goddess, the most gorgeous, beautiful, funny, intelligent, witty, loving woman to ever step foot on planet Earth, and she loved Brett—miracle against miracles, she fucking loved Brett Higgins.

Brett crawled into bed next to Allie, wearing only a T-shirt and boxers. Allie was in a teeny tank and panties. Allie was lying on her side, and when Brett spooned her from behind, she took Brett's hand in her own and curled it around her, placing Brett's hand under her top, on the bare skin of her tummy. Brett didn't know if she was awake or asleep. But she buried her face in Allie's hair and then had to kiss her neck. Just a goodnight kiss, really. But she couldn't resist running her hand up Allie's body, under the thin material of her top. She sucked Allie's earlobe and cupped her breast. Allie was hers and she was here, with her. And squirming under her touch, her caress.

Brett hadn't planned on waking Allie, at least not consciously, but then Allie was rolling over onto her back, and wrapping her arms around Brett's neck. She pulled Brett down so their lips met, and then Brett was lying on top of her.

Brett slid between Allie's thighs, pushing her open, and pushing into her as they kissed. She lay on top of Allie, inside of her on the kiss and feeling Allie all over with her hands. She pushed up Allie's top to cup her breasts, enjoy the soft fullness of them and tweak her nipples between her thumbs and forefingers.

"God . . ." Allie said. "You . . . you enjoyed . . . the bar tonight, huh?"

Brett pulled her up into a sitting position and pulled off her top. "No. I enjoy you. Very much." She lay Allie back down and kissed down her body until she could pull a nipple into her mouth, sucking it, teasing it with her teeth. She pushed her hip bone against Allie while she twisted and pulled on Allie's other nipple. Then she reached down and ripped off Allie's panties.

"Oh, God, Brett."

Brett went down between Allie's thighs, licking up each of her gorgeous long legs in turn, but still pushing them further apart.

She blew up and down Allie's wetness, causing her to squirm and moan. But still, she forced apart Allie's legs, keeping her nice and spread open. She moved in to lick Allie, slowly to start with, then faster, focusing more and more on her clit. At first she caressed Allie's breasts with her hands, then she toyed with Allie's nipples, hard. Then, as she sucked Allie's cunt, she brought down a hand to enter Allie with first one, then two, then three fingers . . .

"God, Brett!" Allie screamed, coming the first time.

Brett rode it out, then brought down her other hand. Without losing pace, she pulled out of Allie and slid into her with the other hand, continuously working her with her mouth. Then she slipped a finger of the first hand into Allie's ass.

"Fuck!" Allie screamed, squirming and writhing. Brett knew she'd like this. With both hands and her mouth, Brett worked Allie, fucking her, eating her, doing her, and they both broke into a sweat.

"You're mine, you know it," Brett growled, sitting up to look down at Allie, both her hands still inside her. "Tell me. Tell me you're mine."

"God, please, Brett . . ." Allie said, her voice hoarse. "I'm yours."

Chapter Ten

Saturday, 7:00 a.m.

Brett woke the next morning with a slight hangover and a cramp in her neck from sleeping on Allie's ass. She tried to roll over, climb up the bed and fall back to sleep, but couldn't. She finally glanced at her watch and realized it was an ungodly hour by any definition. She couldn't believe she had briefly toyed with the idea of joining corporate America, a place where she'd have to get up every day at such an hour.

She stood up and stumbled down to the kitchen, grabbing a two liter of soda and gulping mouthfuls directly from it. She needed to rehydrate.

"Why, I'm surprised you're awake this early," Madeline said, walking in the front door. She had apparently been out on her early morning power walk, an exercise that Brett, who had had to walk just about everywhere until a year after she graduated from college, found absolutely obscene.

Brett turned bleary eyes on her. "Fuck you. I'm going back to bed."

Madeline grinned at her. "You won't be able to sleep. Too much on your mind."

"Grrrr." But Madeline was right. In that big bed, with the sun out and the goddamned birds chirping, Brett tossed and turned, tried pulling the pillow up over her eyes, to block it all out, but still she couldn't sleep. Especially since she didn't want to wake Allie (or maybe she did).

Allie slept on, merely curling into Brett.

Over and over again, Brett made lists in her mind of everything she needed to do—talk to Lauren, Rowan's lawyer, probably Erika again, see if the note she found really was from her. Dave and Diane. Hire folks for their first porno flick. Lease space for the online porn site—live stuff. Then there were the photographers and video folks coming in to get footage for those other sites. She needed to look over all the books. Think about getting in some new and hotter dancers. Talk to some of the Ferndale business owners who had been harassed. Go through the books for all Frankie's holdings. Figure out where they stood and how to make it all make more money.

When she went downstairs, Madeline had made coffee and was putting scrambled eggs, sausage patties, and pancakes on the table.

"I figured you'd need a good breakfast to start off your day." Madeline looked her up and down. "Though I don't know where you really put it all."

Brett knew she ate more than most women and a lot of people wondered, with some hint of jealousy, where she put it all. But she knew she had the height to need a lot of food, and with the way she worked out, she burned much of it off. And muscle needed more calories a day to maintain than did other forms of tissue mass. She didn't want to discount it merely to a really neat metabolism, and she worried about the day she'd actually have to start watching what she ate in order to keep women looking at her.

For now though, she dug into the food with a vengeance, slathering butter onto the hotcakes before pouring on the syrup and taking a generous helping of sausage and eggs. Madeline knew she liked her eggs spiced up with salt, garlic, and coriander.

"You are much too wired to stay here long," Maddy said, as Brett shoveled it in. "I will fill Leisa and Allie in on whatever you need. And what you have thus told me."

"What are you gonna tell us about?" Leisa asked, stretching as she walked into the kitchen with Allie.

"Oh, I have a whole long list of things to do," Brett said. "To help Allie out with the Rowan situation. Like talking with Lauren. Trying to find Rowan. Et cetera."

"I'm in," Allie said. "What's the plan?"

"Okay, so by the time we shower and dress it'll be at least nine or ten. Too early to canvas Ferndale, but Lauren, and Dave, and Diane will probably be up. We can try Lauren first, because she's more likely to be cooperative, especially before noon on a Saturday."

"Yeah, and you'd likely clobber anybody come bugging you before noon on a Saturday," Leisa said, tucking into her own breakfast. "Is there anything you need us to do?"

Brett had hated that she recently put all her friends in jeopardy to keep her own ass outta trouble. She silently signaled Allie over the table that she didn't want these two involved this time. They'd already done enough.

"Oh, do not worry," Maddy said without looking up. "I thought we might visit the Detroit Zoo today, which is thoughtfully located quite near in Royal Oak. Then we have a faculty function to attend tonight in Alma—Dean Guerrero is throwing a mixer to welcome the new director of liberal arts. I think he was worried that too much of the staff that is not working the first half of the summer semester might have been enjoying the break a little too much."

Leisa looked up at her girlfriend. "The Detroit Zoo is in Royal Oak?"

Maddy patted her hand. "Yes, dear, it is. It's where that big water tower is."

"Huh, imagine that." Leisa turned to look at Brett and Allie. "Sure you don't need our help with anything?"

"They wish us to remain safe," Maddy said to Leisa, then, to Brett and Allie. "I anticipate that we will spend tomorrow at home. Feel free to give us a call if you require our assistance."

Lauren and Rowan's house was a neat, older two-story building just southwest of Eight and Woodward near Detroit's northern edge. Brett had grown up southeast of there, in a much less desirable neighborhood. She knew some parts of Detroit were once again becoming decent places to live, but she still wasn't holding her breath about it all. Detroit had too great a stigma for too long for her to trust the gradually increasing property values.

She immediately recognized Lauren when she parked in the street just in front of the house. Lauren, again in shorts and a sports bra, oblivious to the early morning chill that had not yet worn off, knelt in the dirt in front of the house. She apparently had been at it for awhile.

Brett stood behind her for a moment admiring her tanned back and tight ass before finally clearing her throat.

Lauren jumped up, her hand rising to her throat in shock. "Can I help you?" she asked, as recognition began to work its way over her features. Then, "Oh, God, Allie." She threw her arms around Allie.

"I'm so sorry Lauren," Allie said, rubbing her back in what Brett thought could be considered a comforting manner.

Brett gave them a moment, then cleared her throat. They had a lot to do if they were gonna get to the bottom of this.

Lauren and Allie pulled apart. Wiping at her eyes, Lauren said, "I'm sorry, I don't remember . . ."

"Brett," Brett said, reaching forward to shake her hand. "Brett Higgins."

"You met the other night," Allie said. "She's my girlfriend. She's helping with the investigation."

"Thank you so much!" Lauren said, throwing her arms around Brett.

"Anyway," Allie said, "you already know we're looking into Jill's death. We've got some questions."

Sadness rose into Lauren's beautiful brown eyes. Her features weren't as defined as Allie's and carried a softness instead. She was much less the classic beauty as Allie, but there was a loveliness in the slight imperfections. "I still can't believe it," she said, bringing a gloved hand up to wipe the sweat from her brow. "I can't believe Jill's dead, and that they think Rowan did it. I mean, she was right here with me, asleep in bed."

"Do you mind if we go inside?" Brett asked. She liked to see where people lived. It gave her a better idea of who they were. A person's surroundings could often reveal a lot, and right now, Brett needed to know more about Rowan and Lauren.

"I'm sorry, you must think I'm really rude," Lauren said, pulling off her gloves and leading Brett into the house. "I was just trying to keep my mind occupied, doing some weeding. I still can't believe everything that's happened." Her eyes were red and puffy as if she had been crying a lot. That didn't surprise Brett.

The entryway was rather small, fronted by a closet. Off to the left was what appeared to be the dining room, and to the right was a living room. Brett and Allie followed Lauren through the living room and a family room into the kitchen, which was connected to the dining room. Brett realized all the rooms were connected, forming a big circle on the main floor without any real hallways.

"Can I get either of you anything to drink—coffee, juice, tea?" Lauren had led them into the kitchen where she washed her hands.

Brett and Allie accepted a glass of apple juice and they all returned to the living room. It was a nice room, done in fairly neutral colors. A landscape painting added color to the walls. A bookcase lined one wall next to a fireplace. Brett looked at the titles that covered the shelves. They ranged from mysteries to lesbian romances to vampire novels.

"I had been hoping you could help us out," Lauren said to Allie. "When all those cops started calling me when Rowan got arrested . . . well, I was hoping someone could help me."

"It's easier for me," Allie said, "since I'm underemployed. I used to be on the force. A detective. Brett and I are more . . . freelancing these days."

"Oh, PIs?"

"Not quite. Maybe in the future," Allie said.

"So did you used to be a cop as well?" Lauren asked Brett, looking hopeful.

"Hell, no," Brett blurted out, then suddenly realized how she sounded. "I've just been around them so much a little has rubbed off."

Lauren's face fell. "Oh."

"I know it sounds about as useful as trying to teach an old cat some kitten tricks, but they wouldn't've asked me to help if they didn't think I could." Brett sat down on the couch, sipping her juice while she glanced around for an ashtray. She wanted to try to keep this as informal as possible because people often remembered things when the pressure was off and they were given time. Allie sat next to Brett.

"Well, I told the police everything I knew, really." She sat opposite Brett and Allie in a chair. "We left the bar that night, and I had the stupid idea that maybe once and for all we could work out all the problems. I mean, I hated the way Jill's been acting, but I still love her as a friend." She looked away as a tear crept into her eye. "*Loved* her as a friend."

"So the two of you popped by Jill's in the middle of the night, when you were all drunk." This was beginning to stink worse than a rotten tomato forgotten in the back of the veggie drawer in the fridge, Brett thought.

"Yeah, I know, pretty damned stupid, huh?" She got up and

pulled an ashtray and cigarettes out of an end table. "I gave up smoking a few years ago, but . . ." She pulled out a cigarette and put it in her mouth, frowned, and glanced around the room.

Brett stood up and lit the cigarette for her, lighting one of her own as well. "Go on."

"Well, as any idiot could've figured out in advance, things didn't go too smoothly. I still can't believe I took Rowan there." She paced through the room, which might've annoyed Brett a bit if it didn't show off her tanned and toned legs. "Jill was still drinking, and in a mood. She started yelling at Rowan and me, and then she attacked Rowan."

"How'd she attack her?" Brett asked.

"With a fireplace poker." Lauren turned away, obviously still not believing how far Jill had been willing to go. "Rowan pulled her gun then, so Jill backed off. But she took one final swing at Rowan, probably hoping to knock the gun out of her hand. The gun went off, but Rowan didn't drop it."

"Where did the bullet go?"

"Into the wall or a cabinet or something—I really don't remember. I was too shocked and afraid, so I just grabbed Rowan and we got the hell out of there."

"And Jill was still alive when you left."

"Yes, she was." With the back of her hand, she wiped angrily at the tears that now flowed freely from her eyes. Allie found a box of tissues and handed her a few. "I don't know why I was so stupid to even think they could talk like mature adults." She whipped around to look at Brett and Allie. "If it wasn't for me . . ." Her voice trailed off. "If it wasn't for me, Rowan would still be here, not on the run to God knows where. You've got to help us, please."

Brett could smell the intriguing musk of her sweat and look down her tanned chest into her sports bra at her enticing cleavage. She quickly stepped away, going back to the bookshelf to study the neatly framed photos there. "Let me see if I've got this right—Jill's an ex of yours, right?"

"An ex? Yes, the only one I've got." Lauren shivered slightly and went to the front closet from which she extracted a green and white Michigan State sweatshirt. "Or should I say had?"

Allie stepped up. "How long exactly were you two together?"

"Forever. We were best friends—we had practically grown up together." She picked up one of the pictures Allie was looking at, where Rowan and Lauren had their arms wrapped around each other, apparently at some sort of pride rally in Lansing. "Jill and I ended up as lovers when we were fourteen. I guess maybe it was kinda one of those kissing cousins type of things, y'know, we just kinda started fooling around. But, unlike a lot of young girls, neither of us ended up with any intentions of going straight, especially not when we found out there were others like us. We started going to the Affirmations youth group—that's where we first met—you." She looked right at Allie.

Brett's expression must have given her away. Not only had Allie not mentioned the Affirmations connection, but Brett had known Allie for awhile when Allie was still going to the group, and she had no recollection of either Jill or Lauren. Of course, it was like a dozen years ago.

"We didn't really hang out with Allie or anything. After all, she was a bit older and had enough on her hands with that chick she was seeing . . ." Lauren frowned, watching Brett and Allie. "I can't remember her name . . ."

"Kirsten?" Brett offered.

"That's it. God, she was trouble, jumping from one woman to another, made Jill and I quite glad we had each other and didn't have to mess around with all those problems. We didn't go to the group a lot, but it was still nice to know there were other people out there like us." She reached onto the bottom shelf of the bookcase and pulled out a photo album.

Brett was surprised to find she recognized a few faces, like one of her old clerks from The House of Kinsey, the LesBiGay book and gift store she used to manage.

Lauren pointed to him. "I heard he died of AIDS last year." She flipped through a few more pages of photos from some youth group outing until she found one of Kirsten. "Yeah, Kirsten. I wonder whatever happened to her." She was sitting between Brett and Allie.

"She's dead," Brett replied without thinking. There were so many photos in the book.

"Dead?"

"Yeah, dead. Allie shot her, thinking she was me." Brett said. Allie stood and left the room.

Lauren stared at Brett for a moment, then turned back to the album. "And you two are still together?"

Brett grinned at this. "Yeah, I'm a glutton for punishment. Excuse me for a moment, will ya?"

Brett found Allie hiding out by the garage. She wrapped her arms around her. "Sometimes my internal censor doesn't work so well. I say things out loud that I mean to just think. Y'know?"

Allie turned and buried herself in Brett's arms. "Yeah. I just hate our past."

"I do, too."

"You're mine, and I'm yours, and we have to forget all this," Brett said.

"So we go back in and finish?"

"Yeah. I think so."

When they came back in, Lauren was still sitting and studying photo albums.

Brett sat next to her and found herself becoming interested in the photo album, especially when they reached photos of the youth prom of that year, the one she had taken Allie to.

Lauren stared at a picture for a moment, then looked up at Brett. "That's you," she said, pointing. Although the subject of the photo was two other women dancing, Brett held Allie in the background during the slow song. "How long have you two been together?"

"We broke up the next day," Brett said.

"But then you got back together again?" Lauren asked.

"Yeah," Brett admitted with a grin, remembering how Allie had walked back into her life five years later. "We did." Lauren was staring at a picture of herself with Jill. A teenaged Lauren in a pink ruffled prom dress held a tuxedoed Jill close. "What happened to you two?"

"I wanted to go to Michigan State, but Jill's ACT scores weren't high enough. We thought about picking another school, but it was obvious she should be an artist, so she went to CCS—the Center for Creative Studies—and I went to MSU. We figured it'd be four years of hell, but the payoff in the end would be so great, it was worth it. We'd both graduate, get decent jobs, get a house together, and live happily ever after." She touched a photo of Jill in the album. "I'm sure she never forgave herself for that."

"You met Rowan at school?" Brett asked.

"Yeah, we were in the same freshman comp class. She caught me reading some lesbian book one day during lecture—the prof was really boring—and came out to me. Well, I didn't know any dykes up there at the time, so we became friends. We found the queer side of campus together, went to the ALBGS and stuff."

Brett was familiar with the ALBGS—the Alliance of Lesbian-Bi-Gay Students. She had gone to a few of their activities herself when she went to MSU.

"When I first started school, I came home every weekend to visit Jill, but then there'd be parties and things I wanted to do up at campus sometimes, and it seemed all I was doing was living for the weekends. Because I was always gone, I couldn't go out too much with other people, so I didn't really have many decent friends. My second year up there, I asked Jill to come up and visit me more, but she only did once in a while. Well, that kinda pissed me off, y'know—me always having to be the one driving and all that, so I started staying up there without her some weekends. She didn't like that at all, and she didn't like that Rowan and I were friends, either. Like, sometimes she'd call me, and Rowan would answer the phone—because we'd be studying together."

"And nothing was happening between you two?" Brett asked,

having her doubts, but then again, not everyone was like her. She shuddered when she thought of what that meant.

"No, nothing, I swear to God. I loved Jill, even though she was being a royal pain in the derriere. Anyway, she got even more pissed when Rowan would come down with me for an occasional weekend—her parents lived in Grand Rapids so she liked coming to the Detroit area every once in a while. There was a lot more to do here than at her home. By the next year, though, I think Jill started getting a clue, because she started coming up to visit more. She was worried about losing me to Rowan."

"So when did she?"

"After college Jill and I moved in together, renting an apartment till we could get enough money to buy a house. That didn't last more than six months. It was a stressful time—we were both trying to pay off student loans, and she was having a problem finding a job. Plus, she had started trying to sell some of her work, and that really wasn't panning out too well. We broke up."

"How long before you and Rowan got together?" Allie asked. She was leaning forward, sitting on the edge of the couch.

Lauren stopped her nervous pacing and looked at Brett and Allie. "Not very long, I'm afraid. After graduation Rowan found a job down here with the Southfield Police Department, so when Jill and I broke up, she offered to let me stay in her apartment for a while."

"Uh-huh," Allie said, nodding.

"No, nothing like that, though I did find out that Rowan had had a crush on me when we first met, but by this time she said she was over it. I was new to being single, so we started hanging out together even more, and, well . . ."

"I'm sure that gave Jill even more ammunition to accuse you two of having had an affair when you were with her," Allie said.

"Yup. She threw a fit, but she was out of my life, or so I thought. She kept calling us and coming by in the middle of the night. We just about had to take out a restraining order on her."

"So she finally laid off?" Allie asked.

"Yeah, she did. But *finally* is the operative word," Lauren said.

"You know," Brett said, trying to figure out how to phrase it so it wouldn't give away that she had done any breaking and entering recently, "I've heard that Jill had quite a bit of money."

"Yeah, well, she inherited five million from an uncle just before we broke up. He really loved her artwork," she grinned, "and he was gay, so he more than approved of her lifestyle choices."

"Wouldn't that have helped out your financial situation then?"

"That's why I knew it was over—when we were still fighting and arguing all the time even when we had money."

"Do you know anything about her financial situation now?"

Lauren shrugged. "I guess it was pretty good."

"Do you know who inherits?"

Again Lauren shrugged. "I'd assume her brother."

Couple million bucks, and Lauren didn't seem particularly interested? Brett wasn't buying it. "How often did you talk to her after the breakup?"

"Occasionally. Mostly to tell her to leave us alone and that no, I wasn't going to go back to her."

Brett leaned back in the couch, her hands behind her head. "So far you've given me a motive for Rowan to off her—so you'll end up with a helluva lot of money—but do you have any ideas who else might want to do her?"

"Do her?"

Brett grinned and shrugged. "I used to live a life of crime. I've turned over a new leaf—for Allie."

Lauren looked at her and grinned back. "Lemme guess, you're really a writer." She apparently didn't believe a word Brett said, which really was what Brett wanted. No one would honestly ever believe the truth unless they had real reasons to.

Brett shrugged. "So can you think of anyone else?"

"About all I know is there were quite a few women at the bars who really weren't too happy with her. She was a real heartbreaker, and I'm sure more than one woman was hoping to cash in on some of her money."

"Do you know if she'd been receiving any threatening letters or calls?"

Lauren gave her a questioning look. "I don't know. As I said, we didn't really talk too much in the past few years. I had wanted us to be friends—after all, isn't it a rule for lesbians to be friends with their exes?"

"Yeah, so I've heard. What time did you two leave Jill's house?"

"I guess it was about two or so. I know when Rowan and I finally went to bed it was two-thirty, and Jill doesn't live far from here."

"So you two went straight home and directly to bed?"

"Yeah. I was exhausted—too much liquor and too many emotions for one night, I guess. I fell right to sleep and didn't wake up until the next morning when the cops came calling."

"Are you normally such a heavy sleeper?"

"No, not at all. I don't know what happened that night, 'cause I was out sound—but I know that Rowan getting out of bed or anything would've woken me."

"One more question—did you notice anyone hanging around outside Jill's house when you left Wednesday night?"

"Actually it would've been Thursday morning. No, I didn't. I can't help beating myself up over it either. If only I hadn't been so exhausted, I might've noticed something, but I was just thinking about going home and going to bed. I just knew it was stupid to even try to get Rowan and Jill on speaking terms. I will admit, though, that I was thinking about maybe getting together with Jill sometime, for a drink or something, to see if maybe alone I could make some headway on cooling her down. I mean, we couldn't go on forever trying to avoid her just so that she wouldn't make a scene. I just wanted to be friends."

Chapter Eleven

Saturday, 11:30 a.m.

Brett and Allie left shortly thereafter, leaving a business card in Lauren's hands and instructions to call if she thought of anything else or if anything happened that might give a clue as to who was responsible.

It was closing in on noon, and their next stop was Jill's brother Dave's. He lived with his girlfriend across town in Warren in a small home in the southern part of the city, which was the third largest in the state and the home of General Motor's Tech Center. The area was filled with factories and fairly inexpensive homes, partly because it was so close to Detroit and partly because it wasn't too hip.

Brett used to live in the area and knew the people there were pretty damned bigoted, racist, homophobic, and close-minded. Sometimes she'd hear derogatory remarks about eastsiders—

people who lived significantly east of Woodward in cities like Warren, Troy, and Sterling Heights, also known as "Sterile Whites."

"Can I help you?" Diane asked, after she answered Allie's knock. She didn't recognize them from the other night.

Brett suddenly realized that Dave and Diane might not be eager to talk with her and Allie. After all, they probably weren't too fond of the woman who had stolen Jill's girlfriend, that is if they cared for Jill much at all. Brett also realized she had to talk fast before Allie told Diane who they really were. "Yes, my name's Samantha Peterson, and I'm a writer," Brett said.

"Which paper?"

"No paper. We're nonfiction writers working on a project about the survivors of murder, who I feel are usually ignored because people are focused so much on the decedents, as opposed to the effect their loss causes for those around them." She had used the excuse before, and it usually worked, although that was in a small town, not a big city where people tended to be more suspicious.

"You look really familiar . . ."

"Well, yes, ma'am, we have met before, and that's why I'm particularly intrigued by your recent loss. We met the other night at the bar." Brett was really hoping Allie had figured out what she was up to.

"You were the one who broke up the fight!" Diane exclaimed, putting it together. Brett didn't want to deny anything, because then Dave and Diane would clam up if they figured it out on their own.

"Yes, ma'am."

Diane suddenly looked quite uncomfortable. "Well, I guess I should thank you for that. I can't remember whether or not we did the other night, not that it ended up really making much of a difference."

"I'm sorry—"

"It's okay. Nothing any of us could do when it came right down to it. I mean, it's not like there was any reason to think Rowan would ever go that far. I mean, I know Jill didn't always tell us everything, and she had a really bad temper . . ."

"What do you mean?"

Diane shook her head, a single tear making its way down her cheek. "Just what sort of a project is this?"

"It's a book. I already have a few interested publishing houses, but it's not even half done yet. I can't really say too much about it yet, since some of the pieces only come together during the work."

"Oh. Sounds interesting."

"I've already discussed it with a few of my friends at Bantam," Allie said, "and they really want to see it. Anyway, we're especially interested in this case because we were there right before the murder occurred. A murder by any terms is a life-altering event to those immediately around the decedent."

Diane's eyes flashed a spark of light when publication was mentioned, and she invited Brett and Allie in and poured them all coffee.

"I'm sorry," Diane said to Allie. "I didn't catch your name."

"Oh, it's Joan, Joan Lemanski," Allie said. Brett couldn't believe Allie was using the name of a detective who had tried twice to nab Brett for murders Brett didn't commit. It almost seemed as if cops only came into their circle when they were trying to arrest Brett for something.

"Nice to meet you," Diane said, leading them into the rather plain family room with carpeting that had seen better days and walls covered in a dirty, off-white paint that had probably been purchased bulk. Brett plotted out her questioning. Fortunately, she had remembered to bring her notebook to this interview and could play the role to a T.

"Let me see," Allie said, beating Brett to the punch. "You're Jill's sister-in-law?"

Brett sat back, opening the notebook and pulling out a pen.

"Just about," Diane said. "I've been living with her brother for four years now. Ever since we graduated from college."

"Oh, so your full name is?"

"Diane Kristina Emmanuella Fairweather. Dave and I are supposed to get married next year. I was hoping Jill would be my maid of honor, although I wasn't sure if I could get her into a dress for it."

"So you got along well with her?"

"Oh, yes. I mean, she could be temperamental and impulsive, but I think a lot of that was just her being an artist. Underneath she really was quite shy and insecure. She just tried too hard to cover it up, figuring people wouldn't try to hurt her if they thought she was big and strong." Diane was sitting on a loveseat along the other wall. She pulled her knees up to her chin and wrapped her arms around them, the tears running down her cheeks now.

Just as Brett was wondering if Diane was with the right St. Claire, Dave came in carrying two bags of groceries. "Hey hon," he said, looking across the room at her.

"Oh, Dave, I'd like you to meet Samantha Peterson and Joan Lemanski. They're writers interested in Jill's death."

"Really, which paper?" This, of course, launched Brett into a repeat of her entire spiel. She was glad she used the same cover she did in Alma because it was easier for her to remember. She did, however, have to remember how little of the Wednesday night story she had just told Diane.

By the time she was done, Brett was eager to get answers to her questions, but she knew she couldn't just plunge into it. She had to disguise what she really wanted to know, what she was really after, so Dave and Diane didn't become suspicious and toss her out.

But once again, Allie beat her to it. "Now, all I really saw the other night was that your sister, Jill, got into a fight with another woman at the bar."

"Yeah. Rowan attacked her just because she was saying hello to her girlfriend," Dave replied.

"Your sister—was she a lesbian?" Allie asked.

"Yeah, she was. Rowan's girlfriend's her ex. Lauren's her name."

"Lauren. Okay, that's what I'd heard."

To Dave's questioning glance Brett quickly said, "We always do some research before the primary interviews—that way we know something of the situation and don't walk in like idiots."

"We discuss things all along the way, trying to figure out next steps and such," Allie said.

"Oh, that makes sense," Diane said.

"Could you two perhaps fill us in on some of what was going on with the three of them? I understand there were some bad feelings left over from Jill and Rowan's breakup," Allie said. Brett sat back in the couch, taking notes but mostly doodling in her notebook.

Dave raised his eyebrows. "What does that have to do with anything if you're writing about the aftereffects of murder?"

He was growing suspicious, but Brett told herself she really couldn't count it against him because she herself was naturally suspicious of everyone and everything. She jumped in with her line of bullshit. "We're interested in the cumulative effect of the entire scenario. The survivors of a drive-by killing or a convenience store holdup will have a different set of psychological factors to deal with than those such as yourself in which the murderer was known to you—especially since you had witnessed interaction between the two mere hours before the fatal incident." Goddamn, you could tell she had been in business—to be able to come up with such a line of bullshit off the cuff like that. She was quite pleased with herself.

Dave frowned slightly as she spoke, but Brett was happy to see that her fast talking had its intended effect: He didn't question her on it.

"Jill thought Lauren slept with Rowan before they broke up," Dave said. "Instead of looking at the fact that Lauren cheated on her, it made her angrier that Rowan stole Lauren from her when all was said and done."

"Rowan and Lauren met in college," Diane said. "They went to Michigan State, and Jill went to CCS. She was a terrific painter. Have you seen any of her work?"

"Yeah, I think I might've at one of the festivals or something.

Doesn't she have some pretty decent gallery showings or something?" Brett said.

"Yeah, my sister was very talented. But she was lucky 'cause she was able to focus on it. Y'know, devote all her time and energy to it, whereas guys like me gotta work for a living." Brett thought that Dave held a grudge against his sister.

"What do you mean by that?" Allie asked.

Diane sat on the arm of the chair Dave was in, wrapping her arm around his neck. "He's always been a little jealous of Jill's talent."

"Well, that and that people like that, who do weird things like paint and write and shit, well, they can work when they want to and don't have to worry about how many sick days or vacation days they got left."

Neat way to skirt the inheritance issue, Brett thought. They'd just have to get direct with it. She flipped through her notes. "Some of the women at the bar said she always seemed to have a lot of money . . ." she deliberately trailed off, hoping one or the other of them might follow her lead.

"Yeah, she did. *A lot* of money," Dave said. "Uncle Joe left her all his. I think it was around five million. He'd gotten lucky on some stocks through the years."

"He left it all to her? Didn't that piss you off?"

"At first it did, but as soon as I really thought about it, I guess she earned it." To Brett's puzzled gaze he continued, "He was gay and he loved her artwork. So part of the reason she got it was 'cause she's gay, and that didn't seem right to me—kinda like reverse discrimination or something, y'know? Anyways, then I figured she'd paid a price to be gay, like the folks disowned her, wanted to kick her out of the house, and I know she had some problems at school and work because of it. Anyways, his property and a few other things ended up going to a few queer organizations and some other shit, so if he didn't give the money to Jill, he probably just woulda given it away anyway. I mean, if he did split it equally among his nieces and nephews, we probably woulda only gotten a hundred grand each . . ." He trailed off, looked around at the house and grinned, "Not that we couldn't use it, but it wouldn't of been the whole five mil."

Brett thought Dave was too forgiving—especially where five million dollars was concerned.

But then Diane, running her fingers through Dave's hair, added, "Dave makes it sound like he was a lot more upset than he was—but he figured all that out the first day after Jill told us about it. Anyway, Jill was more than willing to help us out. She was going to pay for our wedding."

"So who inherits?"

"I do," Dave said with a wry smile. "Unless Jill changed her will, everything gets split between me and Lauren."

"Lauren?" Allie asked.

Now it was Diane's turn with the wry smile. "Jill still loved her, regardless of all that happened since they broke up. She still would've given anything to get her back." Diane seemed to have a thing for the mystery known as *true love*.

Before Diane could continue, Brett broke in. "Why didn't you two jump in quicker on Wednesday night? Before it got so far out of hand?"

Before Dave could say anything, Diane replied. "The three of them obviously have problems, we wanted them to discuss it, try to work it out."

"I really don't see what that has to do with your book," Dave said.

Brett gave them her best puppy-dog eyes. "It doesn't. I was just curious. I just get so frustrated with all the violence in the world, especially with all the fights at the bars, so as soon as I realized you two were with Jill, I couldn't help but wonder why you let her aggravate Rowan like that when she was obviously so intoxicated."

Dave jumped up. "Listen, that bitch ended up killing my sister, so don't go trying to blame it all on Jill!"

"Calm down honey," Diane said, standing next to him and wrapping an arm around his waist.

"So you're sure it was Rowan who did it?"

"Who the hell else would it of been? She was afraid Lauren would go back to Jill, especially with all the problems they've been having lately!" Dave sat back down. "I guess you'll say because she had such a clear-cut motive makes it a lot different than somebody who just randomly kills."

"Yes, it does. But I understand that Jill was a regular little Don Juan—couldn't one of her many women have gone off the deep end?"

Diane stood and faced off with Brett. "The police arrested Rowan. I don't think they would have come to their conclusions so quickly, especially because she's a cop, unless there were just no two ways about it, do you?"

"No, I guess not . . ."

"Jill just didn't know what to do with all she was feeling about what happened with Lauren—imagine losing the love of *your* life. What would you do?" She was pointing at Brett, standing her down, and Brett felt compelled to back up. "She would've been a fool not to have tried to get her back. She was trying to deal with it the best she could—through her painting. Yeah, maybe she did go a little far and we should've known better than to let her even think of approaching Rowan in the condition she was in, but that does not justify what Rowan did." Brett's back was against the wall. "What you're doing is called blaming the victim, and I don't like it."

"It's obvious that this has touched you both very deeply," Brett started.

"Well, no shit Dick Tracy," Dave walked to stand behind Diane, a hand proprietarily around her waist. "I think it's time for you two to go now."

Chapter Twelve

Saturday, 12:37 p.m.

"Could we have blown that any bigger?" Brett asked Allie as they walked to their car.

"Dave really didn't like us. Actually, neither of them seemed to care much for either of us."

"Well, seems that maybe Diane might've talked if it hadn't been for Dave. Maybe we can catch her alone, later." She almost kicked Dave's old, beat-up pickup on her way out. The thing was a piece of shit. You'd think he could afford better, Brett thought.

"Oh, wait up Brett," Allie said. "You've got something on your shoe."

Brett angrily grabbed the piece of paper from the sole of her shoe, glancing at it only briefly before tossing it on the passenger's side floor. Someone's grocery list, probably Dave's. Yeah, she could imagine Diane needing to write up a grocery list for him to do the shopping. She was impressed, though, that at least he maybe did do some of the shopping.

"Brett. You've got to calm down."

"Sorry, it's just . . . I thought we were starting to get somewhere, and then Dave showed up and blew it all to hell and back."

"We need to focus on what we did learn, and what our next steps should be. Not about what went wrong, but what we learned," Allie said. "Like, would a woman normally discuss her sister-in-law with that much fondness?"

"Yo, we can learn from what went wrong by using that to learn how we can do better next time," Brett said. "But, yeah, I am with you. I'm wicked liking them for the perps. And I mean, Dave—he admitted being initially perturbed with the fact that Jill inherited all that money, but then said he'd come to terms with it."

"But would a murderer admit his own motive? The money?"

"I dunno. He might be admitting it just to throw us off. But if the money is the motive, then we should also think about Lauren. After all, she stood to inherit a tidy sum as well if Dave was right about the will, that they each get half."

"But Lauren was Rowan's alibi. If Rowan's to stand much of a chance on trial, it would be with the reasonable doubt that Lauren would've heard her get up and leave the house that night."

"And your point is?" Brett said, driving them home.

"Lauren seems to be trying to protect Rowan, which she wouldn't if she was trying to frame her."

"But it's not like she's wicked big with the protecting. The alibi she's providing isn't exactly the model of foolproof."

"Yeah, you're right there. This case is a total mess. And that's before we even start to think about all the other possible suspects—like all the women Jill's been with."

"Well, hell yeah," Brett said. "It only takes one woman pissed off enough at being used, and Jill's history."

"Yeah, you mentioned hearing that a lot last night. And, by the way, where'd this entire 'Oh, we're writers writing a book' bit come from?"

"I suddenly realized Diane wouldn't be too likely to help us if she knew we're trying to help the woman the cops arrested for killing her sister-in-law."

Allie shrugged. "Depends. We didn't know till she started talking that she liked Jill. For all we knew, she coulda hated her and been all excited and happy about the murder."

"Fuck. She could be excited and just pretending that she's all wrecked about it. But I figured no matter what, it'd be good if we didn't tell her too much right off."

"Just warn me next time, okay?"

"Yeah. We do need to work out how we're going to approach things if we're gonna do 'em together. I only realized last minute that maybe we shouldn't go at it directly. So I just used the story I used up in Alma."

"I recognized it—your story. Thank God. Or else I might've given us away."

They drove in silence for a few minutes. Brett was glad that Allie'd pretty much read her mind, but there was no way for her to say so, so she just looked over at Allie. "Hey, you 'bout ready for lunch?"

"I can't believe you brought me to a topless bar for lunch!" Allie said, sitting at the table.

Brett shrugged. "We were right here, and they got good burgers."

"You almost had to bribe the bouncer to get us in without a guy."

"But I didn't."

"No, because the owner came up."

"Which means we'll eat for free. What's wrong with that?" The waitress walked up. "Yeah, babe, I'll take the bacon cheeseburger, medium. And a Miller Lite. Al, whatcha want?"

Allie was looking over the menu. "I'll take a chicken Caesar salad—dressing on the side, please. And a Diet Pepsi."

"Coke okay?" the waitress asked.

"Yes, that'll do. Thank you."

"Okay," Brett said, leaning on the table. "We've got Lauren, Dave, Diane, Rowan, and any one of the many, many women Jill did. And then there's that it might be whoever's been harassing queers in Ferndale. So pretty much, I think what we know is that you, me, Maddy, Leisa, Frankie, Kurt, Randi, and Ski had nothing to do with the murder."

"You're cutting down on the suspect list today, aren't you?"

"Well, c'mon—you're the cop. Ex-cop. For all I know the most obvious thing's true—Rowan killed Jill, which means the cops just gotta track her down, lock her up, and keep her locked up."

"Brett Higgins!" Jeff said, grabbing a spare chair at their table and straddling it.

"Jeffie, long time no see."

"It's been a while—ever since those dancers were getting offed, right? Coupla years, maybe? How'd that work out for ya anyway?"

Brett nodded. "I got my man. Woman, actually. Some crazy church type was the one gone nuts and doing the deeds."

"So who is this," Jeff said, looking at Allie.

"Allison Sullivan," Allie said, glaring at him. "I can't believe you call this a *businessman's establishment*."

Jeff shrugged. "It is what it is." He was about to say more, but then he spotted someone across the room. He waved, "Hey, c'mon over here."

Brett looked over to see Tina O'Rourke approaching them. Just what she needed. She stood up. "We're running into each other way too much these days."

Tina brazenly assessed Allie. "Long time no see," she said. "Can't believe you've kept Brett in line all this time."

"Allie, you remember Tina—Jack O'Rourke's daughter."

The waitress brought their food, and Tina sat down.

"It's on the house," Jeff said. Then, to Allie, "So you're Brett's girlfriend, huh? How do you keep a hot fucker like her in line?"

Brett started digging into her food. She looked up at Tina. "I'm not usually wrong about people, so for me to run into you twice in one week like this must mean somethin', huh?"

Tina paused just a moment too long. "I don't have any idea what you're talking about."

"Yeah, right. Then why don't you tell me why you were at my bookstore earlier?"

"I don't think you have any right to ask me that," Tina said, standing and starting away from the table.

"Tina."

"What?"

"I have a bad history with being followed, and I don't like being played." Brett jumped up and wrapped an arm around Tina's waist, securing Tina to herself. She put a hand up to her throat and began gently caressing it. "Two fingers, that's all it takes to cut off all the blood to your brain," she said, pressing gently with her fingers against the major artery in Tina's neck. "Two fingers and you're dead."

Chapter Thirteen

Saturday, 6:37 p.m.

"Baby, do you know where my boots are?" Brett said as she ran through the house in her socks, jeans, and polo shirt.

"They're in the hall closet," Allie said. Things had been rather tense between them since lunch. "And you'd better not be putting them on until we're about to leave."

Brett groaned. Allie didn't want anyone to have shoes on while they were in the house, but Brett hated being reminded about it so much. She went to the study, grabbed her notebook and threw it into her briefcase.

"We're late," Allie said, tapping her foot while standing at the front door.

Brett pulled on her boots. "Yeah, yeah, let's go already."

Although Kurt lived a mere two streets away, Brett still couldn't believe she agreed to walk over. Allie had suggested it, and Brett had reluctantly agreed. After years of walking to and from work because she was too poor to have a car, because her family was too poor to have much of anything, Brett looked at walking as a means of transportation, how she got to and from classes and work when she went to school on the largest campus in the country. It wasn't something she did for the hell of it. And there was a reason Detroit was known as the Motor City—if you had a car, you drove. Even to the 7-11 a block away.

When Kurt answered the front door and saw them, he immediately took a step out and peered behind Brett and Allie. "Are you alone?"

"Yeah," Brett said, immediately glancing around, wondering what he was on about.

"Oh, thank God!" Kurt cried, throwing his hand against his forehead. "I am just not in the mood for another night of watching horror movies with assorted criminals!"

Brett grinned, realizing he was making a joke about the time when she and Frankie dropped a coupla folks off at Kurt's so he could watch over them until they had everything set. "No, this time ya just get an ex-cop and an ex-criminal trying to change her ways. Terrible thing, when perfectly good criminals change their ways."

"Bad girl," Kurt said, leading Brett and Allie into the house. A wonderful smell permeated the air. "You two are late! But, fortunately, I planned on QST."

"QST?" Frankie asked, joining them in the foyer.

"Queer Standard Time. We are condemned by so many others in this world, why should we allow the clock to be one of them?" Kurt replied with a quick three-snap.

After a simply fabulous dinner of steamed cauliflower, dripping in cheese sauce, real mashed potatoes—not the kind from the box—with gravy, and city chicken, which, even after Brett's best "aw shucks," foot-scuffing butch routine, Kurt would say no more about the recipe except that it included pork, chicken, and beef, Frankie and Brett retired to the library for Scotch and good cigars, leaving Kurt and Allie to the dishes and "girl talk."

"So how's the private dick thing going?" Frankie asked, grinning while he put his large frame into the couch after pulling a couple of Cuban cigars out of a humidor.

"Ah, I dunno Frankie," Brett said, rotating the flame of her Zippo below the cigar tip. "Allie and I pissed off two of the people we were interviewing, so they kicked us out. I'm not sure if we're asking the right questions or going about this the right way." She could smoke a cigar if she had to, although she would much rather have a cigarette or a pipe. But she had to give Frankie this little thing, after all he did remember her tastes on just about everything else.

"Oh, c'mon Brett, how'd you figure out who done Liza? Remember, back up in Alma? And what about that mess with Jack O'Rourke? Huh? How'd you figure that one out? And all the other things you've figured out."

"Any moron coulda done those things."

"Liza's was a thirty-year-old murder, for chrissake's Brett. If anybody coulda solved it, then they woulda—thirty years ago! And the morons who were trying to figure out Jack's little mess were ready to haul your ass in on it." He stood, turned Brett away from the window and laid his big, beefy hands on her shoulders. "Did something happen between you and Allie?"

He always could read her. "After we talked to those folks this morning, we went to lunch at Jeff's place and ran into Tina O'Rourke there. Al's been pissed at me since."

"Okay, bud, number one: You took your girl to a strip joint? Number two: What's up with O'Rourke? Is that chick following you or something?"

"You got me. I ain't too pleased about it."

"Whatever. Number three: Seems you're running into problems trying to work with Allie directly. I think you two both like to be in charge on an investigation, so maybe that's where the real problem is?"

"Yeah, I guess you're right, it's just that I'm not sure where this is all heading, and I really should be working harder on getting things together at the theater."

"Don't worry about that, I managed a while without you—"

"So now you're saying you don't need me?"

"Hey, now, you know that's not what I'm saying. All I'm saying is that we won't go under if you wait a couple days before ya start up with those new projects of yours."

Kurt suddenly appeared, his fair hair brushed back from forehead, and he struck a pose with his lean, six-foot body in the doorway. "Is the boy's club ready to adjourn for dessert?"

Frankie pulled Kurt into his arms, rubbing his rough chin against Kurt's hair. "Are you making fun of us?"

"Oh, I would *never* make fun of you big butch types!" Kurt replied with a quick three-snap as he turned and left the room, knowing Frankie and Brett would never miss one of his wonderful desserts, especially not since he had finished the triple-chocolate mousse torte just before Frankie and Brett had left the kitchen for the study.

"I think the butler did it," Kurt said, cutting slices of the torte and pouring after-dinner drinks of Kahlúa and Bailey's over ice.

"Unfortunately, Kurt m'dear, there is no butler," Brett said, taking a sip of her drink. "Could you cut my piece just a little bigger than that?"

"Why don't I just cut three pieces for us and give you the rest?"

"That'll work."

Frankie walked up behind Kurt, wrapping an arm around his waist and lightly kissing the top of his head. "Sure beats pizza, beer, and Ding Dongs, hon."

"Are you complaining about my ding dong?"

Brett chuckled. "Must be nice to have a wife who can cook."

Allie slugged her jokingly. "Why should I learn when you do such a good job at it?"

"Okay, now why don't you fill us in on what's happening? I just love a mystery!" Kurt squealed, mixing his drink with his pinkie.

Brett grinned at Kurt. She never would've thought Frankie would fall for a flamer, but for whatever reason the two of them looked good together. Maybe it was true about opposites attracting—the good, solid Frankie with a fun, flamboyant Kurt and a criminal like Brett with a cop like Allie.

"It's frustrating," Allie said. "We blew it at the St. Claire's today."

"The St. Claire's?" Kurt asked with a raised eyebrow.

"Jill St. Claire's the . . . deceased one," Brett said. "The decedent. Her brother and sister-in-law pretty much kicked us out of their house after a very short time."

"And actually, Diane's just Dave's fiancée," Allie said.

"Well you didn't try telling them you were looking to get the cops' top suspect off, were you?" Kurt said.

"No, of course not," Brett said. "We did find out that the lovely Jill St. Claire, deceased, had a boatload of money—coupla mil at least."

"People have killed for less than that," Frankie pointed out.

"People have killed because they wanted a person's shoes. They'd probably torture for that much money," Allie said.

"So who gets the dough?" Frankie asked.

"Unless something changed at the last minute, it gets divided between Lauren, her ex, and Dave, her brother." Allie said. "Or at least that's what they told us today."

"Dave St. Claire?" Kurt said.

"Yeah, you know him?" Brett said, enjoying the last mouthful of the delicious torte. She was almost tempted to go get seconds.

"Go fer it," Frankie instructed, apparently aware of what she was thinking. He knew her too damn well.

"I work with a David St. Claire," Kurt said, standing and taking Brett's plate. He went into the kitchen and cut her another piece.

"You do?"

"Yeah. And come to think of it, he's been out the past coupla days." He shrugged, handing Brett the plate with another generous serving. "He might be the same one."

Brett sat back, letting a bite of the torte melt in her mouth while she thought. "Maybe you could check into it? See if he is the one?"

"Um," Allie said, "what's your guy look like?"

"Well, duh," Brett said, sipping her drink.

"My Dave is kinda skinny with light brown hair. His nose is a bit big, and he looks rather young," Kurt said. "He's not exactly the friendliest sort in the world, but the woman he's living with—I'm not sure if they're married or what—she's pretty nice. I met her at the Christmas party, and her name is . . . is . . ."

"Diane?" Allie said.

"Yeah. That's her. Duh. That's them. We got the same ones."

Brett and Allie looked at each other, then Allie said, "Tell me about Dave and Diane."

Kurt shrugged. "I don't really know them very well. Dave's been working for us for several years now. He's done pretty well, but he's kinda moody."

"Ya think he could off somebody?" Frankie asked, leaning forward.

"I'm not sure. It's hard for me to think of anybody killing somebody. Remember how long it took me to realize you *weren't* a computer consultant," he said to Frankie. "I'm rather naïve, you see," he continued. "Anyway, David's not boy-next-door material, if you know what I mean." Kurt leaned forward, his fingers steepled in front of his mouth, his chin braced on his thumbs as he stared out the front window. "I remember him being mighty miffed a few years back, and I think it had to do with the fact that his sister inherited a boatload from some relative."

"He said it bothered him for awhile," Brett said, "but he got over it."

"Yeah," Allie said, "but Diane said it took a day—not a while."

"Can you ask around about him?"

"Yeah. I can," Kurt replied with a wicked grin. "But would you like me to?"

Brett growled her reply.

Chapter Fourteen

Saturday, 11:45 p.m.

It was a wonderful night. Not too warm, not too cool. Just right for Brett's jeans, shirt, and combat boots. Kurt had told her this penchant for wearing bulky black boots was a variation of the fag habitué of wearing hiking boots with shorts, but she argued that dykes had always worn clunky black shoes. Regardless, she wasn't wearing shorts.

It was almost midnight, but Brett had no fear when she and Allie strolled down the street back home. It wasn't because she was as stupid and cocksure as she used to be when she was growing up in Detroit, and it wasn't because she knew her .357 could take care of any trouble that came their way. It was because it was a safe neighborhood.

Brett thought about Frankie and how nice it was that he had someone steady instead of his quick fucks in the backroom of the theater. She had always worried about that, about him getting something other than a quick orgasm. Beyond that, she saw Kurt had a relaxing effect on Frankie, and she liked that. Kurt was doing to Frankie what Allie did to her—help her relax so she didn't come to the same early ending as her old boss Rick DeSilva had.

She looked around as they walked and thought of how far she had come. If anyone would've told her when she was growing up that she'd be living in Royal Oak, she would've thought they could read her mind, her dreams, dreams that kept her going all those years ago, the thought that someday she'd get out of Detroit and own her own house, live in an area where she didn't have to fight daily for her very survival.

She took a deep breath and howled at the moon.

"Frankie has such an effect on you," Allie said.

Brett threw out her best grin.

"So what's the game plan now?" Allie said.

Brett shrugged. "You got any ideas?" She was hoping Allie would have some ideas, so they could work separately. She thought maybe Frankie had a point.

"Not really, no."

Brett looked around. For someone used to the nightlife, it was still rather early. If it had been up to her, they might've stayed longer at Kurt's, but she had the feeling that Kurt and Frankie wanted some alone time. "You want to buzz down the Ferndale strip? See if anyone's about?"

"What do you mean?"

"I'm still not writing off the bashers, and they usually use the cover of night so they can hide like the worthless cowards they are." She really didn't like bashers and baiters.

"I'm up for it."

An hour later they were parked in the lot across the street from Affirmations. Brett had pulled on a jean jacket, not for warmth, but to cover her gun. The moon brought just enough light so they could see that the buildings and all looked quiet from their vantage point. Brett and Allie got out of the Jimmy and walked across the street.

The buildings were in a single row, and the businesses shared walls except where a single footpath broke the line. Most of the harassment had targeted the businesses in this area, with only occasional incidences further along the downtown Nine Mile strip, which was only a mile or so long.

As soon as they had checked out the row from the back, they walked along the front and peered in the darkened windows. All was quiet, but this was not a surprise. Although downtown Royal Oak had several well-known bars and restaurants that kept the night-life hopping, Ferndale didn't have many places like that, just one pub across the street from A Woman's Prerogative.

"I'm glad Leisa and Maddy took off today," Brett said. "Well, not *glad* glad, but happy-that-I-know-now-they'll-be-safe glad. Y'know?"

"Yeah. I worry about them too, sometimes," Allie said. "Leisa especially seems a little too gung-ho at times."

"Can be a real good way for her to get into a lot of trouble."

"I trust Maddy to watch out for herself more than Leisa."

"Ya got that right."

"I think Maddy knows it, too. That's why she pulled her home for a few days."

"That must mean Maddy *feels* something's gonna go down. And soon," Brett said.

It was on their third walk around, just as they were about to head back to the car that three teenagers came walking through the alley between the bookstore and Affirmations.

Brett sat on the short wall that stood between the two buildings and lit a cigarette. Allie stood a few feet away, looking around.

"You ready for this," Allie whispered.

"I'm ready to throw down," Brett said, wholly aware of the way the three boys were looking at them when they stopped and leaned against a building. Two of them lit cigarettes and the flames of their cheap disposable lighters danced in the moonlight. She knew just when they stopped leaning and approached her and Allie. One of them wore boots that clicked on the sidewalk, but the athletic shoes of the others were quiet as a G-string hitting the floor.

"Damned dykes," one murmured.

Could Brett have gotten this lucky that she found the guys on her second night out? She had expected them to be males. After all, only the most obnoxious of all women would ever follow up on such hateful thoughts with any action.

They were only a few steps away, and their voices grew louder as they hurled more invectives at them. She stood and turned, looking at them. The tallest was a lanky lad a few hairs taller than her. They were probably about sixteen or so. What the hell were they doing out at this hour? It was nearing on two a.m.

"Damn dyke," the tallest said, looking Brett over first, then Allie. "You out recruiting or something?"

Brett walked right over the wall, her graceful body and long legs taking her right up to him. "Whatcha gonna do about it, asshole?"

His friends gathered around her, circling her like a pack of wild dogs closing in on their prey. "Too damned many of you around here."

With a swift movement Brett reached up, grabbed him by the back of the neck and threw him to the ground. Allie was already kicking the knife out of the hand of another before he could even flip the blade out. As it tinkled on the pavement, the third boy took off running.

Brett flipped around to kick the guy with the knife onto the ground. She picked up the knife and knelt on the first guy's back, pinning him to the ground. "You have any idea who's been leaving little love notes at the bookstore here?" she growled into his ear.

"No, no I don't," he said, his voice trembling.

"What about you?" she asked the other kid who was shakily getting to his feet.

"No, no, ma'am."

Brett reached into the back pocket of the kid she knelt on and pulled out his wallet. Extracting his ID she said, "If I ever hear differently, the cops won't have a chance to get to you." Then she let them go.

"I don't think they had anything to do with it," Allie said, standing with her arms crossed in front of her. She sometimes let Brett do the dirty work, since she was trying to keep her record clean.

Brett watched the boys' retreating forms. "If they did, they didn't have anything to do with the murder. Even a drunken Jill could've taken out two of 'em. Three or four maybe. I saw her fight Rowan at the bar. At the least there woulda been signs of a fight at the house."

"Yeah. I'm with you on that. So what should we do tomorrow?"

They walked back to the car. "I think we need to check out the stores here," Brett said. "Look into the hate mail they've been getting. It's probably these morons, but I think we need to finish investigating this possibility. Cross out everything that we're sure did not cause Jill's untimely demise."

"Makes sense."

"I'd also like to find out if Rowan, Jill, David St. Claire or Diane Fairweather had or have any guns registered to them." She paused, thinking of everyone who was involved in the case. "And add Lauren to that list."

"And you want to know this because?"

"Shooting in the dark. If someone was planning on blowing her away, they'd need a gun to do it."

"But do you think they'd actually have it registered then? If they bought it to kill somebody?"

"Listen, sweetie, I'm pissing in the wind right now. If you have any ideas or anything, feel free to throw them out here, but right now I know damned well I'm grabbing at straws."

"I love you, Brett," Allie said, stopping her just before they got into the car. "I don't ever want to go to that restaurant—not ever—

again. Never. But I am glad you're helping me with this." Brett was glad Allie was being bold enough to bottom-line their issues of today.

"I love you, too." Brett suddenly realized how often she said this out of mere reaction, then she realized that she really did mean it and feel it. "I'll do everything I can for Rowan."

"Thank you."

Brett suddenly thought of something. "Can you drive? I wanna give someone a quick call." She tossed Allie the keys.

"Sure."

Brett pulled out a business card and dialed the number on her cell.

Artie picked up the phone on the first ring. "Hullo."

"Brett Higgins here. I was wondering if you could verify that both Lauren Bianchini and Dave St. Claire will become quite rich from Jill's death."

She could picture him grin. "Yeah, I kinda thought about that myself. And Davey-boy and his fiancée Diane are each other's only alibi."

Interesting that he was so ready with this information. Especially at this hour of the night, Brett thought. What was he even doing awake? "And you know that Lauren and Jill were exes, and there had been some scenes between them before," Brett said. If she gave him some tips, he might be more willing to share with her if she came up with some things for him. "Jill was a sexual player—screwed a lot of women, then left them. Which means that quite a few women could've been moved to commit a crime of passion against her."

"I like the way you think, kiddo." She woulda busted him in the chops for calling her that, if he had actually been there. "And for that, I'll tell you that the ballistics test came back—the bullets in Jill and her house came from Rowan's gun. All of 'em."

"And when you guys got Rowan's gun, how many bullets were missing?"

"Four." She didn't need to be told that was how many bullets were fired. "Which I don't like. It's all too pat."

When she hung up, she quickly filled Allie in on who she'd called and what he'd said.

At home, they determined that tomorrow, Allie would still look into who had guns registered to them and ask around at the stores on Nine Mile. She'd also see Randi about background checks on all the major players in this little drama.

Meanwhile, Brett planned to drive up to East Lansing. They didn't have many leads, and she figured checking out the old alma mater wouldn't be a bad idea. After all, it seemed as if this entire drama had started up there. Brett had gone to school there, Allie hadn't. So this division of labor made sense.

Chapter Fifteen

Sunday, 10:15 a.m.

Brett slept in the next morning, enjoying the relaxation and rest as well as the dreams in which she was her old self, dating multiple women at the same time. She figured she could at least enjoy it in her dreams, even if she was now in a monotonous—er, monogamous—relationship with a woman she loved so dearly that she could no longer act on her impulses the way she once did.

After a shower she threw on jeans, boots, and a tank top emblazoned with a rainbow flag that Allie bought her when they went to San Francisco Pride. When she put on her watch, she glanced down at her MSU class ring. She hadn't bought one until almost two years after she graduated because she couldn't afford it. Of course, she'd had to replace it when she lost it years later.

There was something bothering her about the little trio of Lauren, Rowan, and Jill, but she couldn't quite put her finger on it. Allie had agreed with the story Lauren had given her about how she and Rowan had gotten together, and Dave and Diane's few remarks about it gave further support to that version, but Brett still didn't feel right about it.

She put her class ring on her right hand. She planned to drive up to East Lansing, home of Michigan State University, and try to find anyone who could remember Lauren or Rowan from their college days.

She opened the little box that held what little jewelry she owned: A few black leather cockrings and a couple of chains and simple necklaces, like one made of stainless steel that was a circle behind a triangle suspended on a leather cord. She selected one of the cockrings, a fairly slender one with protruding studs, and snapped it onto her right wrist.

Brett didn't care too much for personal ornamentation. She didn't wear jewelry or have a single piercing or tattoo. She knew these things could easily assist identification, and she did not want to be identified. She did, however, like her women to wear jewelry, and she loved Allie's navel ring. Back in the old days, though, Brett wore a cockring on her wrist every day. She thought it provided an interesting contrast to her usual attire of tastefully coordinated suits—just enough to throw people off balance.

Thankfully, the only person in the kitchen this morning was Allie apparently having her second cup of coffee.

"Eggs or omelet?" Brett asked.

"Oh, I had cereal. I wanted to get going, but you looked so cute asleep, I figured I'd let you sleep a while longer."

Brett put the eggs back in the fridge and just poured herself a coffee. "I'll grab something from Mickey D's on my way then."

Allie walked up behind her, wrapped her arms around Brett's waist and hugged her from behind. "You've got a lot of driving to do, so maybe that's best."

Brett turned around in Allie's arms. "I'll keep my cell on. Give a holler if you learn anything or need anything."

"Will do."

They kissed. Brett thought about everything else they could do, but . . .

Allie parked across the street from AWP and Affirmations and looked around, feeling a brief chill when she remembered the night before. She hoped those punks had learned a lesson but still couldn't help feel her anger build when she considered what might've happened if it had been someone else they harassed that night, someone not quite so prepared.

Pushing it out of her mind, she glanced up and down the row of businesses, figuring there were three she should stop and visit. There was Affirmations, the LesBiGay community center; Just 4 Us, which she thought carried Pride items or something like that; and of course, A Woman's Prerogative—AWP. She decided to start with the latter first, so she jumped out of the vehicle and quickly walked across the street.

She was barely inside the door when she was charged by a white and black bullet of a dog. Allie knelt to scratch behind her ears. She, for Allie just knew a lesbian store would not have a little boy for a puppy, was a Boston terrier who didn't even reach her knees. Mostly white, she had a few large black patches, one draped rakishly over her eye.

"Bella!" a woman from the front of the store called. Bella briefly interrupted her inspection of Allie's shoes to glance around. Allie had only been in the store a few times, although it had been around for quite a few years, but she always liked the general feel of it. Places had a feeling to them, and this one had a good one.

"Is there anything I can help you with?" a woman said, approaching her. She was one of those dykes whose age one couldn't quite place—she could be anywhere from thirty to fifty. Her short hair was salt and pepper, and her slightly stocky body gave a sense of strength and reliability. The small smile on her lips made Allie think she probably had a wicked sense of humor. She was the older dyke Allie could imagine Brett turning into.

Allie stood. "I certainly hope so. My name's Allie Sullivan, and

I'm trying to get some information on the recent harassment of local businesses."

A cloud passed over the woman's face. "I . . . um . . ." she reached down and picked up Bella, scratching the pup's tummy, "I think you should probably talk with the owner when she gets back." She looked at Allie with smoky gray eyes. "I'm just watching the store, and the dog, for the weekend."

"What happened?" Allie asked. The woman looked away. Allie reached out and touched her arm. "What happened?" she asked again in a softer voice.

"You said your name's Allie?" she said, and when Allie nodded she continued, "I'm Karen. I help out occasionally around here. Anyway, it's nothing big, just a bit of magic marker on the front windows." When Allie looked around her toward the front of the store she said, "I already cleaned it off. And there was another note."

"Have you turned it over to the cops yet?"

"No. As I said, I'm just helping out, I figured—"

"Could I possibly see it?"

"Well I dunno—"

"Karen, I was outside here last night and some kids attacked me and my girlfriend—"

"Omigod, you weren't hurt, were you?" Karen asked, giving Allie a quick once-over.

Allie smiled. "No, but I think they were."

"Did you report it to the police?"

"No, but I have the ID of one of the kids," she reached into her pocket and pulled it out, handing it to Karen. "If they want to follow up on the vandalism. But could I see the note?"

Karen studied the ID Allie handed her for a moment, then went behind the counter and pulled an envelope out from underneath the computer. Allie glanced at the computer to see some sort of inventory program running on it before taking the envelope from Karen's hands.

The envelope was plain white. Inside, on a piece of plain white paper was a handwritten note: Ferndale don't want no dykes!

The words—a neat, flowing cursive—were written in blue ink. It was a heavy script, written so deeply she could feel the imprint of the letters on the underside of the paper when she held it.

"Have they all been handwritten?" Allie asked in amazement. Especially with all the computers today, writing a note on a computer would be the most anonymous way. Either the basher was getting bold—or stupid—by laying it out in identifiable handwriting.

Karen shrugged. "I'm not really sure, but I think so."

"Can I take this for a few minutes? Just to make a copy of it?"

"Oh, I can do that for you right here—we've got a fax machine that makes copies. It won't be the greatest reproduction in the world, but . . ."

"I'm sure it'll work." When Karen handed her the copy, Allie again studied it. Something about the writing was familiar. Another strange thing was its preciseness, its neatness—it looked more like the writing of a woman than a man, certainly not the sort of guy who'd write a note like that. Of course, here she was stereotyping and jumping to conclusions herself, no matter how much she raged against doing so in the real world. "Could I see that ID again?"

"Yeah," Karen, who had been closely watching her, replied and handed it over the counter.

The signature was nothing like the handwriting of the note. Allie handed it back with a quick thanks, then headed to the front of the store while Karen dealt with the latest inventory shipment, opening boxes and unloading them while she compared them with the invoice before she shelved them.

Allie could barely make out the outline of the words Karen had just cleaned off the front window. It looked like someone had scrawled, "Dykes!" She was surprised they'd manage to spell it correctly. Standing outside, running her fingers over the slightly damp glass, she tried to imagine who had done it. She could picture the jerks from the night before doing it, probably just after she and Brett made their last circuit of the buildings. She cursed under her breath, wishing she'd caught them at it. She might've been all up for and joining in the beating of their asses if she had seen them doing this.

She went back in the store to look around. The place wasn't huge, but it was nicely stocked, floor to ceiling, with books of all sorts and videos and DVDs for sale and rent—a few of which were Fatale pornos, she noticed with a smile. She recalled that one of them had a wonderful fisting scene in it. Perhaps she should pick one up.

That was when she noticed the store was now carrying a small selection of toys. "How long have you been selling these?" she asked Karen.

"What? Oh, those," Karen paused, looking away. "Oh, it's been a few years now."

Although there weren't a lot of them, they were of a fairly high quality and a fairly broad range—from dildos, vibrators, and lubes, to harnesses and butt plugs. Allie was impressed.

Allie left the store and walked down the street just a few buildings to Just 4 Us, another queer shop, but she learned nothing further from the fags there, nor from anyone at Affirmations.

She called Randi and arranged a meeting at Randi's office. There they'd have free reign of the computers to look into anyone they wanted.

Chapter Sixteen

Sunday, 1:36 p.m.

It took Brett ninety minutes and a stop at a drive-thru to get to East Lansing. She headed directly to Michigan State University's student union, where what she had known as the ALBGS (Alliance of Lesbian, Bi, Gay Students) was housed, though she was sure that with all the changing political currents in the queer community, it had a new name by now. She remembered all of the fighting that went on to get bisexual students acknowledged the last time the group changed names, so she well imagined that someone was still feeling left out of the group. Hell, for fuck's sake, it could be that hets felt left out of the queer community these days—and were mightily pissed because of it.

She grinned while she went through the traffic circles, and thought of how many people from out of town she had directed through them just to laugh at their inevitable confusion. MSU was the nation's largest land-grant university, its grounds extending far beyond the campus proper. There were large chunks of land used for sheep studies and research and other agricultural and veterinary pursuits that quite confused Brett. All of this simply ensured that a few times a year, the entire campus reeked of manure while they did some strange ritual involving animal excrement.

But it was quite a beautiful place, with built-in parks, large areas of landscaped greenery, and a river that was home to tons of ducks during the summer. At other times, various pieces of furniture would be floating in the river, especially during CedarFest, the annual party in Cedar Village, one of the many apartment complexes in and around MSU. To call it a party would be an understatement—it was more of a mass hysteria, complete with people hanging from trees and burning beds and mopeds and anything else that looked as if it could make a really cool bonfire.

Brett struggled to find a parking spot since hordes of students were returning to campus after a weekend trip home. She called home on her cell to check for messages while she cruised around. Allie'd left a message. Turned out Rowan had both a service revolver and the .25 Beretta registered to her. Brett assumed the latter was her off-duty gun. The only other one on their list of who had a registered gun was Dave St. Claire who, coincidentally, also had a .25 Beretta registered to him. Brett imagined he'd be one of those guys who wanted a big gun, not something small and concealable like the Beretta.

She finally found a spot and pulled into it, then quickly raced up the four flights of stairs to the headquarters of the ALBGS. Fortunately, someone was in.

"Can I help you with something?" asked an earnest young woman. Her head was neatly buzzed cut, her muscular arms furry in the pits, and she was clad in a black tank top and short jean cutoffs. Birkenstocks on her feet, of course. Brett was never one of these earnest young women who were fighting the good fight and who aimed to make a difference. Back then, she didn't have the time, money, or ambition to do so. She was too busy working too much, wanting to come out of school in a different position than when she entered. She wanted to live on the other side of the tracks.

A lot of these women were born on the right side of the tracks and made a conscious choice to try life the other way. Many also had never known that privilege, but were so firm in their beliefs and hopes and ambitions for change, they were willing to do almost anything to make the world the place of their dreams.

But Brett knew change didn't come easy, that it took a lot of work to create change. Perhaps even she, by forcing men to learn to respect and admire her, forced some baby steps toward change. And the lipstick lesbians who were accepted in the mainstream—when they came out, people realized that the stereotypical "uniform" of lesbians was just a figment of their imagination.

But activists had their place. This earnest young woman didn't recognize Brett, so she was apparently going under the assumption that Brett was taking a brave first step in coming out.

"Don't be afraid, we're just here to help," she said.

"Hey, hon," Brett replied, laying a hand on the shorter woman's shoulder, "I've been out since you were still on the playground. I'm here trying to get some info on some friends who went to school here and were involved with this group."

"Oh. Well, I've been here a while, so maybe I can help you. My name's Kathy." Kathy offered a hand and Brett took it. "Who're you looking for?"

"Rowan Abernathy and Lauren Bianchini. They graduated just a coupla years ago." She glanced around the walls of the room, at the posters from *Desert Hearts* and *Torch Song Trilogy*, as well as framed newspaper pages and a flyer from a play called *And Divided We Fall*. Apparently, MSU had actually sponsored a comedic play about gays in the military just after Brett had graduated. Brett turned her attention to the framed local newspaper pages, looking for a picture of Rowan and Lauren. She found one.

"There, that's them," Brett said, pointing to two women with their arms wrapped around each other in the background of a *State News* shot.

Kathy leaned in closer. "Nope, sorry, don't know them."

Brett was about to ask if she could think of anyone who might remember them, when a tall, redheaded, slender man flamed into the room.

"Stephen!" Kathy yelled, "Just the man who can help us!"

"Oooo! Girlfriend! You know how I love to help dykes in distress!" Stephen threw off a quick three-snap just before wrapping an arm around Kathy's hips.

Kathy pushed him back a bit. "Do you know these two?" She pointed to the picture of Rowan and Lauren that Brett had pointed out to her in one of the old clippings. "Stephen's a grad student, been here quite a while," she said to Brett.

"PhD, actually. Let's see if I can remember—Lauren and Rowan . . . Lauren Bianchini and Rowan Abernathy. They were so the cute couple!" A playful grin slid across his face. "And Lauren could raise such a ruckus!"

"Huh?" Brett said. Lauren said they hadn't gotten together till a while after college.

"She only looked sweet and innocent. Under that exterior, she could be a real hell-raiser. Like, she could fake anybody's handwriting, so one time she—"

"No, I mean, they were a couple?" Brett asked.

"Oh, yeah, big time. It was quite a mess for a while there, too. If I recall correctly, they started dating before Lauren really broke up with her ex." He suddenly stopped and looked at Brett. "What's this about anyway?"

"I'm investigating a murder." Both Stephen and Kathy looked appropriately shocked and curious. "Lauren's ex, a woman named Jill, was recently killed, and they think Rowan did it."

"Rowan? Kill somebody? Are you crazed, girl?" Stephen said. "Rowan could never kill anybody. Be real."

Kathy took a step back from Brett. "Does this mean you're a

cop?" Brett could almost sense the little hairs going up on the back of Kathy's neck.

"No, I'm not. Don't worry. I'm just curious—I don't think the cops down there are looking into things well enough." That's it, Brett thought, play on their feelings toward cops. She knew how to do that. "So they, Rowan and Lauren, were dating while they were still in school?"

"Yeah, you can see right here in this picture they've got their arms around each other."

Kathy glanced at her watch. "Listen, I've gotta get going, there's a bunch of us meeting to coordinate a trip to Festival. Do you think you can handle the phones for a bit?" she asked Stephen, not even waiting for his response before she left.

Stephen quickly closed the door behind her and pulled two chairs together, ready to gossip. Brett knew this was her signal to get ready to flame in order to get the most faggy gossip possible.

"So what's the four-one-one?" Brett said with a grin when she sat next to Stephen.

"Well, we were all undergrads together, and we naturally fell in together 'cause we'd all been out forever. Just a bunch of naïve freshmeat." He grinned at his own joke. "But it was obvious to anybody who paid any attention at all that there was something going on between them."

"Did you ever hear of Lauren's ex, Jill?"

"Oh, yes. She came up here a few times. And that's when the good stuff started. We all had to act like Rowan and Lauren were just friends, though I'm pretty sure everybody knew the truth. I mean, of course I hated the charade, but what can you do? I mean, I didn't want to be involved in any sort of dyke drama, if you know what I mean?" Brett nodded eagerly, wanting him to continue. Thank God for fags like Kurt who had taught her how to play the game. "But then Jill started coming up more frequently, and the next thing I knew, Lauren had even given up playing the game and trying to convince her they could last forever and ever. 'Course, you and I know no such thing can exist. Nothing lasts forever." He gave a deep sigh.

Brett put an arm companionably around his shoulders. "Bad love affair."

"Too many to count. What's a poor lil' fagboy to do?" He shrugged. "But you don't care about my little trials and tribulations . . ."

"C'mon, you don't seem the sort to give up so easily."

Stephen stood up. "Easily? Easily you say, my dear? Oh, my, nothing in this life is ever quite as easy as you'd like it."

Oh great, Brett thought, just what I need—someone else who speaks in riddles. Maddy liked to mind fuck like that. But she decided not to say anything.

"Nothing ever lasts. Look at Lauren and Jill. I mean, when Lauren started school here, she would go on and on about Jill and how much she missed her, but then . . . but then, I'm not sure when it happened exactly, but Lauren and Rowan became . . ." He let his sentence trail off, finishing instead with a little eyebrow waggling to indicate that Lauren and Rowan became more than friends.

"So what did you think of them? Rowan and Lauren and Jill—did you ever meet Jill?"

"Humph. Jill. Stuck-up little prig, especially once she got all that money."

"Once she got all that money? I thought she didn't inherit until after they all graduated?"

"Not at all. In fact, when push came to shove, she tried to use it to keep Lauren."

"But Lauren wasn't impressed, I take it."

"Again, humph. When push came to shove, the only one of the bunch I really liked was Rowan, she wasn't going to change or sell out for anybody. The other two can rot in hell where they belong as far as I'm concerned."

"What're you talking about?"

Just then, the door opened and Kathy returned. "So did you

two get all the gossiping out?" she asked. Several other blatant dykes followed her into the room, making themselves comfortable on the chairs, sofa, table, desk, and floor of the small room.

"Not quite, dear," Stephen said, standing. "But we'll toddle off to the bar, where proper butches and fags belong, and leave you all to your safe space." He turned to Brett and said, "Michigan. Such the festival. Such the drama."

"Why don't I drive?" Brett suggested and led the way to her car after Stephen made a quick call from the pay phones in the lobby of the building. She wondered why he hadn't just used the one in the office, but supposed he had his reasons—like not wanting Kathy to know who he was calling.

"That would be a fine idea, especially since I don't have a car. Doctoral blues, you know."

"We going to Five-O-Dive or Paradise?" Brett asked, referring to the two gay bars in nearby Lansing, the former being the nickname for 505, the lesbian bar, and the other primarily a boy bar.

"Since you're with me, why don't we do Five-O-Five. Although I wish we could go to Trammpps, the old bar. That closed quite a while ago—they took down the entire block to make room for a parking garage. Of course, they chose the block that had the gay bars and porno shops on it. Probably part of some sort of clean-up or something—getting rid of the undesirable elements."

They finally pulled into the parking lot of Five-O-Five and went in. It was early Sunday and the place was nearly empty. Although Brett had been here quite a few times before and had known that Trammpps was closed, going back into the old ALBGS office, hell, being on the campus and being mistaken for a student made her feel like a student again.

They sat next to each other at one of the long folding tables away from the dance floor. Stephen glanced about as they sat. Brett was curious—Stephen told quite a different story than Lauren had about the relationship between Lauren and Rowan and the timing of both that and Jill's inheritance. Of course, Brett thought, he might just be a gossiping little fagboy, but it was worth it to find out what else he might know.

"So you don't like Lauren or Jill," Brett began.

"So you're not a cop."

Brett sat back in her chair and sipped her beer, lighting a cigarette. "No, I'm not. Why do you ask?"

"Curious. Then who are you?"

Give to get. The basic rule of life. It never changes no matter where you are. "A friend."

"Of whose?"

Brett studied Stephen for a moment, his elegant fingers gently tapping the edge off his cigarette, his legs properly crossed in their neatly pleated khaki slacks, well-polished loafers on his feet. His red hair wasn't quite as perfect as the rest of him and was somehow reassuring in its unruliness. A hint of a smile danced across his lips, as if he were daring or testing her—but how or why?

His clear, green eyes reflected light from the nearby video screen when he again glanced around the bar, and she finally answered. "Rowan once saved my girlfriend's life, when they were cops together."

"So you *are* a cop."

"No, I'm not. My girlfriend *was*. And she's got me helping her to clear Rowan."

"But who the hell are you then?"

Brett grinned. "The truth?" Stephen nodded. "A crook. A criminal. That's why she wanted me to nose around—because she knows I'm familiar with working around the law."

Stephen sipped his beer and studied her, as if weighing something heavily in his mind. Brett suddenly remembered Lauren flipping through photo albums, and realized that on one of the pages that Lauren passed was the reason she felt a sense of déjà vu with Stephen: His picture was in there. Not only in some of the photos of the march, but also as Rowan's date to her senior prom. Like hell he met them both when they all came to school here.

There was only one other person in the bar, some old guy sitting a few tables away, solemnly drinking his beer. Stephen had paid close attention when he entered, and it was that entrance that halted Stephen's wandering glances. He didn't quite seem Stephen's type, nor did he seem the type to frequent a dyke bar.

"I was wondering why you were talking with me, why you chose to speak to me, but I think I know now," Brett said, brusquely standing and quickly walking to the old man, who hopped to his feet just as Brett approached.

Brett roughly grabbed his hand and spun his retreating figure to face her. She put a quick hand to his cheek, to rub off some of the facial makeup that created a ten o'clock shadow across his face, then pushed back the knit hat that covered his head.

"'Bout time we met *again*—Rowan." Stephen was at Brett's side, trying to pull her off Rowan, but with her free hand, Brett grabbed Stephen by the neck, and in a gentle, careful movement, she used his own height against him and pushed him backward onto the floor, bringing Rowan down with them.

"Hey there! What's going on?" the bartender yelled, coming out from behind the bar.

"Nothing, nothing at all," Brett said before saying to Stephen, "Why don't we go back to your dorm where I'm sure you've been hiding Rowan."

Rowan looked down at Stephen, still locked in Brett's grasp, and nodded.

Chapter Seventeen

Sunday, 4:57 p.m.

Stephen lived on the fourth floor of the west wing of the graduate student dormitory. It was a great hiding place for Rowan. No one would ever believe two people could cohabitate in such a small room. And being on an upper floor gave Rowan the entire building as a hiding place if need be. If anyone showed up, she'd know it before they got up to the fourth floor, and she could take off and avoid them.

When Brett was a freshman, she lived in Hubbard Hall, an undergrad dorm with suite-style bathrooms. One night, after beer kegs had been outlawed in the dorms, her floor didn't have a resident assistant to keep track of what they were up to. That night she had seen a keg wandering up and down the floor as the building's management tried to track it down. The managers would go into one room and the keg would go out through the bath to the adjoining room and out into the hall to another room down the hall. Brett could easily imagine a person doing the same thing.

Brett had a difficult time finding a place to sit down. Clothing was strewn over the pull-out bed that doubled as the base of the couch, dirty dishes covered the more flat, stable surfaces, and books and papers were piled in stacks all over the floor.

Stephen quickly cleared the clothing off the bed and pushed it into a pile on the floor, albeit with a wince, so that he and Rowan could sit next to each other on it, and Brett could sit on the single desk chair. Before she sat, however, Rowan ensured that both the door to the bathroom and the outside door were locked from their side.

"So just who are you?" Rowan asked as soon as she was satisfied with the arrangements.

Brett didn't sit in her appointed seat, instead she stood, knowing she was taller than either of the other two. "I think I'm the one who should be asking the questions."

"How do I know you're not just out to get me?" Rowan countered.

" 'Cause the cops haven't raided yet, nor have I slapped a pair of cuffs on you." Brett grinned. "And just know that I look at cuffs solely as an erotic toy."

Rowan carefully looked Brett over, that statement seemingly keying off her memory. "I know you. You're the woman from the bar the other night. Allie's girlfriend."

"Yeah, I'm the one who kept you from finishing her off then."

"What do you mean by that?"

"I mean that at least I kept you from doing her in a public place. That's about the only way you coulda made things harder on yourself."

"You think I did it?"

"Witnesses. At least we saved you from that. This way we might actually have a chance of getting you off."

"Listen, I didn't do it!"

"Then why the hell did you run? You might as well have put up a neon sign saying 'guilty' with a big arrow pointing at yourself."

"I'm not guilty."

"Then convince me. Tell me what happened that night."

"Jill was all over Lauren, like she always is when she finds us together—"

Brett held up a hand. "And," she said, stressing the word, "I want to know the truth behind your little ménage à trois."

Rowan visibly flinched at that particular phrasing. "Stephen, do you think you could go out and get us some beer?"

"Don't . . . why . . ."

"Please, Stephen, just do it—trust me," Rowan implored, leading him to the door. She locked it behind him, leaned against it and looked at Brett. "Can you at least tell me your name?"

"Higgins, Brett Higgins."

"Like Bond, huh?"

"Yeah. But I play on the other side of the fence, and I drink Scotch, not martinis. So you gonna tell me 'bout you, Lauren, and Jill?"

Rowan sighed, sitting on the couch with her head in her hands. "Lauren and I met in ATL—freshman English—and hit it right off. I respected her relationship, though I kept wishing things were different. I knew from the first time I met Jill that they weren't right for each other. I could make Lauren much happier. Stephen and I are from the other side of the state—we went to our high school prom together—"

"Yeah. I figured that one out already." Rowan looked at Brett in surprise. "Lauren let me glance through some of your old photo albums yesterday. Go on."

"So I visited Lauren that summer at her folks' house. As a *friend*, I stayed with her. I knew Jill was jealous of me, 'cause sometimes that year I'd answer Lauren's phone when she called. And I felt guilty, because I did have a crush on Lauren, but nothing happened, even when I realized how much Lauren was putting into their relationship and how little Jill was. I mean, Lauren was always going back home on the weekends—missing out on all the parties and fun things to do up here then. So I started flirting with Jill when we were together, just to make her feel more comfortable with me, and so that she wouldn't notice just what I was feeling for Lauren."

"So you flirted with Jill. Didn't look like that the other night."

"Well, there's more to it than that." Rowan paced, digging through the stuff on the desk for something. Brett finally offered her a cigarette, and she gratefully accepted it. "You see, sophomore year, Lauren and I moved in together, as roommates, that's all, honest . . ."

"But?"

"But . . . but she stopped going home so much, mostly because of me. I convinced her that Jill needed to start putting a little more effort into the relationship if it was going to work."

Rowan was nervous, and Brett had the feeling she'd never told this story to anyone before. "So when'd all that change? When did you first fuck her?" Brett prompted.

"I didn't fuck her! We might've been drinking that night, and things just got out of hand, but I never fucked Lauren, I loved her far too much for that! Love her too much for that." Brett simply stared at her, slowly flicking her Zippo. "We got home after an ALBGS dance one night. Although there wasn't alcohol there, we had a few drinks before and after with friends. We got home and fell into the lower bunk, my bed, and she started teasing me about some woman who was at the dance that night. She wanted me to say I liked this woman, and I wouldn't, so she started tickling me, and I finally told her I didn't like this other woman 'cause I liked her." Rowan was lost in her reverie, remembering that night. "She stopped tickling me then, and looked at me instead. It was like she was looking at me for the first time, though I knew she *had* looked twice before—after all, I wouldn't've held on that long if there wasn't some return interest as well."

"So you two became lovers your sophomore year?" This was

very different from what Lauren had said, and Brett wondered who was telling the truth. Rowan only nodded, and Brett asked her next question. "What about Jill?"

Rowan looked down. "It was near the end of the year that this happened, and I had to work near my home, and Lauren hers, so she was supposed to break it off with Jill that summer."

Brett took a deep breath, she wasn't used to this, but she sat next to Rowan and put an arm around her shoulders, gently comforting her, or at least tried to. "What happened?"

"I don't know. Whenever we talked, she said things were complicated. I even went over there for a weekend, and had to hang out with the two of them, like they were the couple. When we moved back in together for our junior year, she told me she was still in love with Jill, but she was in love with me as well."

Brett finally understood the hatred and rivalry between the two women. "When did the three of you first go to bed together?"

Rowan was quite embarrassed by it, but Brett recommended she tell it quickly since Stephen was bound to return shortly.

"Jill had come up for the weekend. I'd told Lauren I hated it when she did that, because then I had to find somewhere else to sleep, and it burned me to know that Jill was doing her in our room."

"So what happened?"

Rowan went to the window and stared outside. "We went out to the bar that night. I was supposed to stay with somebody on a different floor, so we all went and came back together. Lauren was in a flirtatious mood that night, and . . . well, I had to go back to the room to get my stuff before leaving those two alone for the night. Lauren poured me a drink, insisting I stay for one last one." Rowan turned to face Brett, a slight grin dancing across her face. "I remember it like it was yesterday," she whispered. "Lauren went to Jill, straddled her lap, and began necking with her. When I started to leave, she told me to stay. She looked right at me and told me she wanted me to watch." She looked right into Brett's eyes as if daring her to say something about it. Brett didn't.

"Lauren likes to wear sports bras, and she was able to take off her shirt and bra in one movement."

Brett remembered the way Lauren looked just hours before in her sports bra, and then thought about what she'd look like without it. She liked the image. "And Jill just went along with it? Invited you to join them?" She hadn't imagined that Rowan would give her so many details but knew there must be some reason for it.

"Not quite." She took a deep breath. "She got off Jill and asked me if I liked what I saw. She took me by the hand and sat me down next to Jill on the couch. She turned the lights down low and put on some soft music. I don't know what Jill was thinking, but I was wondering what Lauren was up to. I was kinda dazed, y'know, from drinking, but watching a half-naked Lauren was definitely turning me on. I almost forgot Jill was there until she moved, but then I could tell she was getting turned on, too."

Rowan was confessing. She wanted Brett to understand how all of this had begun. That's why she was telling it all—it was a cleansing.

"She turned to us, her hand on her zipper, and asked if she should take off her jeans, asked if we wanted to touch her. I was going fucking nuts—I mean, she had me so turned on, but then I was jealous because Jill had just been making out with her, and it almost seemed like she wanted me to watch Jill touching her." Rowan was quite animated now, and Brett could understand, could empathize with everything she was saying.

But Brett could also imagine the cute, soft brunette butch in front of her, the cocky Jill with her long auburn hair and sensuous curves, and the teasing Lauren with her long legs, blond hair and tanned skin going at each other. It was quite a vision.

Rowan's voice dropped to a whisper, and she leaned in close to Brett. "She told us she wanted us to kiss. I couldn't believe it. I mean, I knew she had asked me what I thought of Jill and if I was attracted to her, but . . . I suddenly realized she had probably done the same with her, and . . . and honest to God, I just turned to Jill, not meaning to *do* anything, but . . ."

"But what?"

"But then suddenly we were touching each other, kissing . . . her tongue was in my mouth. And Lauren was there, too."

Brett imagined sharing Allie with another woman—but, of course, it'd have to be with another femme. No way could she share her woman with another butch. But watching her with a femme—long, slender curves pressed against the same, with Brett there guiding them, helping them along . . .

"That was in the spring. Up until then, Lauren had kept us both around, saying she loved us both and couldn't stand to lose either of us. What can I say? I was young and stupid so I believed her."

"Sounds like you're kinda pissed about it."

Rowan grinned and shook her head. "I can't believe I'm telling you all this."

Brett grinned back. "I have that effect on some people. It's probably 'cause a lot of folks realize I've seen way too much to really judge anyone for anything."

"It was college, it was fun and different, like smoking pot. We were experimenting with sex. All that summer we kept at it—in fact, even through our senior year we were a threesome. During the week, Lauren was mine. Some weekends she was mine, some Jill's, and some we all were each other's."

"What happened then?"

"I made Lauren choose. I couldn't go on like that. We got along when we were together, but Jill . . . Jill would've driven me nuts. We had no future as the three of us—but I loved Lauren, and I did care about Jill, deeply."

"One fucked-up situation."

"You got that right. But Lauren did choose me."

"You won."

"Yeah, I did, but Lauren did hold it against me for breaking up such a good thing."

Stephen returned, and Brett accepted a beer. She knew Rowan wouldn't continue talking about the threesome, so she switched to her other topic of interest. "Can you take me through the night that Jill died? Tell me absolutely everything, no matter how stupid it seems."

"We were at the bar—"

"Why?" Brett asked, sitting back, ready to absorb all the details. She wanted to picture it all quite precisely in her head. "I mean, why did you decide to go to the bar that night?" There might be some little detail that would make everything fall neatly into place. Yeah, right, she thought. And ducks burrow into the ground for the winter.

Rowan shrugged. "Lauren felt like dancing. We don't normally go to the bar on weeknights, but we hadn't been out for a while, so . . ." She took a sip of her beer and looked at Brett as if she might have some answers. She didn't, so Rowan continued, "Anyway, once we were there, we started mingling, running into old friends, all of that. I don't know how long Jill had been there, but I caught her brother pointing at us a coupla times. I didn't pay much attention, because I was drunk. Lauren wasn't drinking much though, because she was our designated driver." Rowan smiled and shrugged. "After all, she was the one who wanted to go out. I was trying to ignore Jill, 'cause the last thing the woman ever needed was any reason to get in our faces."

"Why didn't you leave when you knew she was there?"

Again the shrug. "We didn't like running from her all the time. I thought maybe she'd leave us alone if we just ignored her, but then she tried to cut in when Lauren and I were slow dancing, and then became more persistent. That's when you walked in, so to speak."

"Okay, now correct me if I'm wrong here, but it seems that ignoring someone and pulling your gun on her are two totally different things." Brett still couldn't believe the incredible stupidity of the action—anyone pulling a gun in a bar was really stupid, but a drunk cop pulling a gun on a drunk civilian in a bar was absolutely idiotic.

"Listen, I already know I fucked up big time, I don't need you judging me as well. You remember the jacket Jill was wearing that night? Didn't you wonder why the hell she was wearing such a thing on such a nice night?"

"Are you saying she was packing?"

"Hell, yes. Damned gun laws'll give anybody the chance to buy one. I saw it earlier in the night when she tried to cut in while we were slow dancing, so when she came back out and grabbed Lauren's ass, I stepped in, pulling her away. She tried to punch me in the stomach, but I grabbed her arm and pulled it behind her back. She tried to yank away, but I held her. People started surrounding us, and she reached for her gun. I knew if she got her hands on it, she'd start shooting, so I pulled mine out."

"Do you remember what sort of gun she had?" It had to be a pretty small piece, maybe a Beretta. Since Brett hadn't noticed it, it really was quite possible it was something small—something like a Beretta.

Rowan chuckled. "Yup. Somehow she knew exactly what I carried, so she got one just like it. A twenty-five caliber Beretta." Brett must've given her some sort of a look, because she quickly added, "I don't know why she'd want a gun—or one like mine, all I know is that she had the same sort I have as my off-duty weapon."

"Okay, so the party broke up, and Lauren took you home, stopping en route at Jill's—"

"I told her it was a stupid-ass idea. I mean, Jill was obviously drunk. Of course, when wasn't she?"

"So it was Lauren's idea?"

"Yeah, she said this had to stop and maybe Jill would be more understanding if she didn't have such an audience to save face in front of—like she did at the bar."

"Now that's a fucked up idea," Stephen said from where he sat, highlighting passages in a textbook with a pink highlighter. He abruptly returned to his work without waiting for an answer. Brett had almost forgotten his presence in the room.

Rowan leaned forward to whisper in Brett's ear. "I think what happened at the bar turned Lauren on. I think she wanted . . . I think she wanted us both that night." She looked down, a tear running down her cheek. "Sometimes, if Lauren had a coupla drinks, she'd get really, really horny."

Brett noticed Stephen pause in his studies, his marker poised over the page in mid-motion.

"We rang the doorbell, and Jill answered almost immediately. She must have seen us coming. She led us right in and poured each of us a drink. I was thinking that was the last thing she needed, more to drink." Rowan looked up at Brett. "Lauren was almost trying to play both sides of the fence, flirting with us both and reminiscing about some of the good times we had together. But Jill wasn't hearing any of it, she got real evil, saying how Lauren dumped her and shit. Then she got right into Lauren's face, telling her about some of the women she's fucked lately. About how many women wanted her and what she's got while Lauren's stuck with me. How much pussy she's eating. She started touching Lauren, and, well . . . I thought maybe that was what Lauren wanted, but she started crying and looking real scared, so I told Jill to back off. That was when Jill flipped and grabbed the fireplace poker."

Stephen now listened with intense interest. Rowan would've noticed this, except she was so into the story, she had probably forgotten he was even there. Brett couldn't imagine that she was so freely saying such incriminating things in front of him after it had been obvious that she didn't want him to know about their little three-way affair.

Rowan held up her right hand, which sported an angry red mark across the palm. "I tried to grab it, but then she started on me. Lauren yelled, so Jill held off a second. I pulled my gun, thinking to scare her, but she hit me on the arm." She pulled up her sleeve, showing another deep, angry welt. "The gun went off. I knew we had to get out of there then, so I grabbed Lauren and ran."

"You just ran?"

"Listen, I just shot a hole in her wall. I mean, the woman was already pissed, and I really knew then that that was not the time to go trying to talk sense to her."

"Did she follow you?"

"Nope. I thought that was lucky, but . . ."

"Did you notice anything when you got there or when you left? Any cars in the street or anything? Anybody outside?"

Rowan shook her head. "Not that I saw. And for chrissake's Brett, it's Ferndale—tiny garages, small driveways—of course there were cars on the street."

"Do you remember any of them?" Brett asked, thinking about Rowan's neighborhood. It was nighttime when this happened—just as it was when she broke in. There were lots of cars when she broke in, but it still seemed a quiet neighborhood.

She had almost forgotten what she asked by the time Rowan answered. "I think there was some black sports car in the driveway across the street. Two doors down, on Jill's side, was a beat-up old pick-up. Across the street, in the street, was an old yellow T-bird, some fancy red truck, and a black Jeep." She shook her head. "That's all I can remember."

That was a pretty amazing memory feat, Brett thought, but then remembered Rowan was supposed to be able to remember such stuff, being a cop and all. "And you two went right home and to bed?"

"Yes. Now I wish we'd gone out for breakfast, like we sometimes did after the bar, but no such luck. We went right home and to bed. Next thing I knew I was being hauled in for questioning. I didn't know what was happening, so I let them take my gun and everything."

Brett sat back on the couch and stared up at the ceiling. Something here was missing, some key fact. "You said Lauren didn't have much to drink that night?"

Rowan shook her head. "No, she was driving. She had one, maybe two at the bar, and then another at Jill's."

Chapter Eighteen

Sunday, 8:01 p.m.

On her drive back from Lansing, Brett thought about everything Rowan had said. What she found especially interesting were the variations in Rowan's and Lauren's stories of that night. Rowan said Lauren drank a bit, but not too much—she was the designated driver. But then she said that Lauren got horny after a coupla drinks, causing Rowan to think maybe Lauren wanted a threesome with Jill. Again.

It was Lauren who took them to Jill's, wanting it over once and for all. Aside from that, the night was about as she had already heard about it, with the additional fact that Rowan admitted to shooting the gun, but then she left right after that, because she thought it'd be best to work it through when they were all sober.

What remained was why Lauren had lied about their relationship. And that Rowan wasn't breathing a bit about Jill's inheritance—she thought all the money came from lucky breaks in the art world. Or at least that's what she was claiming.

Brett needed to know exactly when Jill inherited. She needed to find out who was telling the truth and who was lying. Probably the only person who could tell her whether Lauren or Rowan was telling the truth was Jill, but Jill was dead.

Brett thought she should also breeze by Jill's place and see if she could ID any of the vehicles Rowan saw that night, see if any of them shouldn't've been there. See if any of the cars Rowan mentioned were nearby. Damned good thing it hadn't happened on Friday night when the street was lined with cars. Of course, that would've meant a greater likelihood of a witness. Someone to verify something, anything.

She realized only a few people would be able to get her the information she needed about Jill's inheritance—her attorney, the cops, and her banker. Dave and Diane would probably know, but she wasn't sure if she could trust them anymore than she could anyone else. Besides, they probably wouldn't tell her anything anyway.

She wanted an objective opinion. And she knew how people could have connections within their industries—after all, look at her and some of her competitors. They could battle fiercely, but they could also help each other out. The banking industry certainly had to be more civil than them. And she just happened to know a banker that might have some knowledge of Jill's monetary situation.

But Brett wondered about the real reason Lauren wanted to stop by Jill's that night. It seemed rather consensual as to the expected reason, but Rowan did offer the idea that Lauren wanted to return to the days of their threesomes.

Brett tried to imagine the way the night went—how Lauren and Rowan showed up at Jill's, how Jill poured them all drinks and how Lauren started flirting with both Rowan and Jill. Brett liked the thought of Lauren being a flirt, toying with both women. She could imagine her casually brushing up against them, touching them, maybe letting her blouse fall open a bit so she could lead Brett's hand under it, under the sheer satin of her bra, against the warm flesh of her soft breast with its rock hard, puckered nipple.

Brett quickly shook her head, trying to pull herself out of her reverie to pay attention to the road. Things sure did turn on Lauren, though. All three of them, in fact. Jill was dead, Rowan was wanted for murder, and Lauren didn't get laid. Really, Lauren lost both her lover and her ex that night, 'cause Rowan was going up for murder—unless Brett did something.

Brett was still hot from Rowan's descriptions of the ménage with Jill and Lauren as well as from her vivid imagination, so she needed to drive by Jill's house and scope out the cars, she thought to herself. Her next stop would be the bar to see if Erika was there, because maybe she'd know something about Jill's financial situation—after all, she was a banker. Brett knew it was a long shot, but she wasn't exactly dealing with many clues right now.

She almost had to force herself to drive by Jill's house, but didn't see any of the vehicles Rowan had mentioned seeing that night. But it was still early, so people could be out and about, especially in this weather. This nice weather.

Brett pulled over, got out of her car and walked around. She didn't find anything new—but she could've sworn someone in the house across the street was watching her through the curtains. Meanwhile, Brett thought Allie could work on the money situation and research it. But the will hadn't been read yet. There were still a lot of maybes floating out there. Too many, in fact.

Brett considered going home, strapping it on, and taking Allie enough for two women. She'd take her first in the living room, then tie her to the bed and do her again. She could almost taste Allie right now, taste her sweetness, her sweat, and feel the softness of her skin. Brett adjusted herself in the seat, turned the music up louder and went home.

After talking up the folks at the shops on Nine Mile, Allie'd gotten in touch with Randi, hoping to dig around a bit more into the background of all the players in this little drama. Even though

Randi had a girlfriend now, Allie knew she was still interested in her, and it made her feel sexy. And younger.

"I think we've got everything Brett wanted," Allie said, standing and stretching. She noticed Randi's gaze on her, and she liked it. She stretched a bit further.

"So Allie . . ." Randi said. "Ya wanna get a burger or something?"

"Yeah, sure. Let me just leave a message for Brett. Let her know what's the what and all, y'know?"

Nobody was home. Allie didn't answer her cell. Neither did Frankie or Kurt. Brett was just packing all aces tonight.

She turned on the surround sound and threw on some dancing tunes. She grabbed a Molson Ice out of the fridge, lit a smoke, and went into her study. She needed to go to the bar, but with each sip of beer she got more and more cocky, doing her moves through the house while she nuked a frozen dinner (had to keep her strength up) and jotted down anything she had thought of during her drive before she forgot.

She needed to go to that bar and play a role. She needed to get Erika to tell her everything she knew. But Erika wanted to play, and she wouldn't just volunteer the information.

Allie still wasn't answering her cell. Allie was with Randi. But Randi now had a girl—Ski. Joan Lemanski.

Fine. Brett thought Erika wanted her, Brett, to play a part, and she would. She'd do just what Allie wanted and get information about this entire mess. She went upstairs to their bedroom and stripped off her jeans and athletic briefs. She opened a drawer of the bedside table and pulled out her favorite black leather strap, carefully inserting a thick, lavender dildo into it before donning it and putting her briefs and jeans back on. She checked herself in the mirror, adjusting as needed, turned off the lights and left.

Erika wasn't at the bar and neither was Amber. Brett had learned through the years that enough money could get her just about anything she wanted, even their address because as it turned out, they lived together.

Yeah, she could've just called them, but that wouldn't have been as much fun. And, anyway, she hated leaving messages. Really, what could she say, "Eh, yo, this is Brett, and I need some more dope on Jill's finances?" Lame.

Brett felt a twinge of excitement when she drove up to the quiet suburb of Troy. Erika had definitely made her desires known the other night and although she played hot and cold, Amber had been quite clear as well.

Brett found their two-story house without much difficulty. She walked up to it, figuring from the flickering lights in the front window that someone was up watching TV. She knocked on the door, and Amber answered, wearing only a short, black satin bathrobe. Her skin was still pink from the shower, her long red hair still slightly damp.

"Oh, you," she said, turning and walking back into the room, allowing Brett to follow her if she chose to.

Brett walked in, refusing to allow the cool attitude get to her. "Is Erika here?"

"Who is it?" Erika asked, entering the room attired in her own short satin bathrobe, but this one was red. She immediately broke into a smile. "Oh, hello." She let her gaze slowly wander up and down Brett's figure, saying as well as words just what she was thinking.

"How'd you get our address?" Amber asked, sitting on the couch and brushing out her long hair.

Erika shot her a look. "Can I get you something to drink?"

"Yeah, that'd be real nice. You got any Scotch?" She let her gaze do its own wandering.

"Make yourself at home, I'll be right back."

Brett sat in the middle of the couch next to Amber, who moved away from her. Brett hoped it would be a decent Scotch. She turned to look at Amber, who returned her look with one that could kill. Erika came back into the room carrying a bottle of Glenfiddich and three glasses. She sat on Brett's other side. Brett picked up the Scotch, poured, and handed each woman a glass, her fingers lingering with Erika's, while Amber took her glass coldly. Her eyes held a teasing within their depths, though.

Brett sat back and sipped her drink. "So what're you two doing at home?"

"Remember, we're regular working girls, nine-to-five, during the week," Amber said, turning a bit to face Brett better, her robe falling slightly open in the process. Brett found their robes far more tantalizing then their costumes of the other night. Those were mere clothing, whereas these were teasing challenges—things to be taken off. "What brings you here at this time of the night, though?"

"That same case I was working on the other night."

"Oh, is that all?" Erika said, running a finger down Brett's arm.

"It was a good enough excuse, I thought."

"And what is it you need to know tonight?" Amber asked, not touching Brett, but not moving away either, even as Erika began caressing Brett's thigh.

"Just some more information on your friend Jill."

Amber watched closely while Brett traced the collar of Erika's robe. "She said the information was just an excuse to come over here," she said.

"And what are you willing to do to pay for this information?" Erika asked, running her nails down the bare skin of Brett's neck.

Brett reached over, putting a hand at the back of Amber's head, and pulled her in, gently running her lips over hers. Amber let out a low groan as Erika leaned in closer to Brett.

"Hmmm, so the big, bad butch did come to play," Erika groaned into Brett's ear just before she ran her tongue over it.

"Well, I do need to find out exactly when Jill St. Claire inherited that tidy little fortune."

Amber pushed herself away from Brett, but Erika continued to explore Brett's muscular thigh with her hand. "Don't worry, she's just playing hard to get," she purred into Brett's ear.

Amber stood and walked across the room, lighting a cigarette. She leaned against the wall, staring at Brett, her long, bare, legs stretched out luxuriously, spread just enough to be inviting, welcoming. Her hands dangled from her sides, her satiny robe opened down past her breastbone, revealing a tantalizing terrain of soft, tanned flesh.

Brett turned toward Erika, pulling her into a long, deep kiss, her tongue pushing its way into the warm, sweet wetness of Erika's mouth. The touch of Erika's tongue sent a jolt flying through Brett's body, right down to her cunt. She ran her hand over Erika's satin-covered breast, enjoying the smooth softness, the way her nipple hardened to push up against the material and Brett's palm. She gently cupped the breast, wanting to feel flesh against flesh, but also enjoying the wanting.

"So can you get me the information?" Brett asked, her voice a low growl.

"Tomorrow," Erika whispered between moans as Brett's tongue flicked down her neck toward her collarbone. "I'll call you tomorrow from work. She was one of my clients. That's really how we met." The sentences were punctuated by long pauses when Brett's tongue flicked, when she started pushing Erika's robe open a bit more, revealing more of her chest, of the swell of her breasts that now outlined the island of flesh on either side.

Brett looked away from Erika, toward Amber, when she slowly pulled the tie on Erika's robe. Amber's gaze was glued to hers, only leaving to briefly flicker over Erika's exposed skin. Brett was beginning to see what Amber's interest was in all of this game.

Brett crossed the room in two strides, grabbing both Amber's hands in one of her own and pressing them above her head against the wall. Amber gasped in surprise while Brett quickly extinguished her cigarette before pressing her body tight against the wall with her own, her thigh pushed hard against Amber's pussy while her tongue forced its way into Amber's mouth.

Brett rubbed her thigh up and down between Amber's legs, her tongue exploring the warm mouth. Amber struggled lightly against her, but that was only part of the game, because she didn't try to bite Brett's tongue or struggle nearly as much as she was capable.

Erika sat on the couch, casually watching, her still untied robe just covering a few crucial areas while she smoked a cigarette. Brett turned to her, and she put the cigarette down.

Brett abruptly left Amber to sit next to Erika. Amber leaned against the wall, breathing deeply, her face flushed, her nipples hard. Brett watched both women when she slid her hand under the material of Erika's robe up near her collarbone, then slowly slid it down to cup her breast, feeling the hard, taut nipple strain against the palm of her hand. Brett watched Amber squirm against the wall when she traced down Erika's chest, then followed across her lean stomach.

She finally pushed Erika's robe open enough to reveal her left tit in its lush entirety. Without looking at Amber, who was now lightly licking her lips while still pressed against the wall, she addressed her, "Do you want to touch Erika? Or do you want me to touch you like this?" She gently sucked the exposed nipple, then turned to Amber. "Or maybe you just want me to take you hard and rough and that's why you're playing these games."

Amber's gaze locked with Erika's. She walked across the room, leaned over Brett and gently brushed her lips over Erika's while her hand found the exposed breast and caressed it, tugging at the nipple, playfully brushing it back and forth.

Even as Brett suddenly realized Erika and Amber had never before been together, Amber pulled back just enough so Brett could see their tongues tangoing in the open space between their mouths.

Brett loved seeing these two very attractive femme women touching like this, so intimately, and like they meant it. She could feel her own cunt heating up, and she wanted to join them.

She put one hand on Amber's leg, raising the robe when she followed the curve of it up to the nicely shaped ass, enjoying the bare skin and curves. Her other arm was draped around Erika's shoulders, and she moved that to push the rest of Erika's robe back, revealing her other breast.

Erika and Amber both turned to look at her, Amber's hand still on Erika's breast. Erika reached over, took Brett's hand and, after lightly caressing and holding it for a moment, she placed it inside Amber's robe on her tit.

Amber stood up straight, undoing her robe with one hand while leading Brett's hand from one breast to the other, then down between her legs to the thin strip of red hair. "Does this answer whether or not I want you?" Brett's fingers gently probed her slick, wet cunt while she arched and moved against the hand, breathing deeply while Erika watched.

Erika stood, her own robe falling fully open, and pushed the robe off Amber's shoulders. Amber closed her eyes and shifted, as if she were uncomfortable with her own nakedness, but then she reached over and pushed Erika's robe off. Brett stood up between them, her arms wrapped around each woman, her hands filled with naked flesh.

Erika leaned over and kissed Brett, her hand undoing Brett's shirt buttons while their tongues danced together. Brett pushed Erika into a sprawled sitting position on the couch while Amber pulled off Brett's shirt and sports bra. Erika's legs were spread wide, and Brett kissed, licked, and nibbled her way up the thighs as Amber tried to undo her belt, her breasts pressed against Brett's now bare back, but Brett pulled her up to also kneel between Erika's legs.

"Oh, God," Erika moaned when they pulled her lips open and first one tongue, then the other ran the length of her labia, from vagina to clit. Brett slid a finger into her, then Amber followed, each woman gently probing her, pulling in and out while exploring inside of her.

Brett moved up to nibble on her nipple, keeping a finger inside of her, while Amber ate out her friend, almost unable to withhold any more, her tongue wildly flicking back and forth.

"Oh my fucking God!" Erika came in a wild shudder, her muscles squeezing tightly around Erika's and Brett's fingers.

In a few seconds she was kneeling down with them, her body pressed against Amber's.

"Now it's your turn," Brett said, lifting Amber roughly off the floor and all but throwing her onto the coffee table with her legs spread wide. Brett stood at the foot of the table and Amber's eyes grew wide when she took off her belt and snapped it, but then Brett tossed it aside and undid her zipper and again Amber's eyes grew wide, but her cunt arched into the air when Brett pulled out the dildo she had been packing.

"Oh my God," Erika whispered, taking in the size of the tool. Brett knelt between Amber's legs, and with both hands she spread Amber's lips wide, then roughly slid her thumbs up and down her soaking wet cunt. No need for lube here. She grinned, then leaned over Amber, guiding the dildo up into her. They stared right into each other's eyes while she gently guided it in and out, in and out.

Erika stepped up behind her and ran her hands up and down Brett's now almost entirely naked body, feeling the hard muscles, her hips moving up and down with Brett's as Brett drove into her friend, deeper and harder with each thrust.

Amber's eyes seemed to challenge her as they matched tempos—Amber arching up as Brett drove in. But Amber tried to hide what she was feeling, which became increasingly impossible as she neared orgasm.

"Brett, oh God, Brett," she finally moaned, breaking her eyes from Brett's and turning her head to the side, "oh baby, ride me like a thoroughbred!" Erika moved to kiss Amber as she finally wrapped her arms around Brett, their bodies glued together even though her tongue was dancing with another woman's.

It was only when Amber came that she wrapped both her arms and legs around Brett and kissed her hard and deep.

Erika knelt patiently beside them until Amber collapsed back onto the table, spread eagle. Then Erika ran a hand down Brett's back, her fingers fanning out to caress the side of her breast. "Now don't even go trying to tell us you're stone."

Brett stood, and Erika was right there, pushing Brett's pants, shoes and socks off. Then Amber was nibbling on her nipple while loosening the strap-on. Erika leaned over to kiss Amber, then both women were running mouths, tongues, and hands over Brett's now naked body.

Brett was already wet, turned on not only from fucking them both, but also from seeing two femme women touching each other and from the strap that rubbed against her own cunt when she drove in and out of Amber.

She gasped when both women's hands found her sopping pussy at the same time, her knees weakening while also wanting to spread further. She slowly sank to her knees. Each woman had a hand on her cunt and a mouth on a breast. She groaned then lay down on the floor, pulling Erika up to sit over her face. Amber took the hint and her mouth traveled down Brett to her spread legs.

She didn't plan on Amber entering her, let alone using her own dildo on her, albeit manually out of its strap, but when she felt it pressing against her, she couldn't speak nor back away because Erika, still crouching over her, held her securely in place.

Her mouth lapped at Erika, her fingers probing around to curve up into her, while Amber flicked her clit back and forth with her tongue, slowly working the dildo in to totally fill her, then pulling it back out, leaving her wanting more, even though no one had ever done such a thing to her.

She pulled her fingers out of Erika and dove in with her tongue instead, pushing it up inside of the other woman while Amber continued lapping at her, matching her rhythm with the dildo, pushing its great girth up inside Brett, making her squirm while she tried to concentrate on making Erika come first.

Erika began to buck on top of her, and she held her in place by wrapping her arms around her sleek thighs, following her cunt with her mouth, her tongue.

"Oh, God, yes!" Erika screamed, coming in an array of twists and turns till she collapsed in a writhing heap on Brett, and Brett could finally give in to the sensations spreading up through her stomach, down her legs, making them quiver, the heat licking its tongue up from her cunt as Erika began to bite at one of her nipples and roughly twist the other while Amber worked her over further down.

She neared the edge, her entire body shaking while she wished she could spread her legs further, give the women even more of herself, allow them to touch her even deeper. Her breathing was struggled as she gasped for air, and then she could feel it deep inside, building out . . .

"Oh, fuck!" she screamed.

Chapter Nineteen

Monday, 1:13 a.m.

Several hours later they lay entwined on Amber's king-size bed, both women laying their heads on Brett's breasts, her with an arm around them each, with each of them laying a leg over hers. Their sweat-covered bodies reeked of sex, but each satisfied from multiple orgasms.

"Goddamn, I need a cigarette," Brett said. Amber sat up on one elbow and lit a single cigarette, apparently expecting them all to share. Once Brett took it, Amber leaned over to lingeringly kiss Erika, running a hand down over her long, slender body.

Erika moaned and shifted her position a bit. "I'll die if I come anymore tonight, sweetie." Although she couldn't dance very well upright, she did the horizontal mambo very nicely.

Brett knew she shouldn't spend the entire night, and she also knew there was no way she could hide what she'd been doing all night.

She was still enjoying this far too much. "Erika, do you have any idea about when Jill inherited?" Their bodies were so nice, warm, and soft against hers.

"Mmmm," Erika replied, "at least we got your mind off business for a few hours." She rolled onto her back, taking control of the cigarette so that Amber had to light another one for her and Brett. "I was just looking through the file—since you were asking questions the other night, but I'm bad with remembering dates."

"Was it before or after she finished college?"

"Before," she said, then, more slowly, as if it was coming to her. "It was during the summer, between her sophomore and junior years. I remember because at that point, I was working two shitty jobs so that I could take a thankless internship the next summer to gain some experience before graduation. It made me a little green when I found out she got so much money so young."

Very interesting, the same time Lauren gave Rowan the runaround about the breakup.

"If I were you, I'd be looking at whoever inherits," Amber offered. "Jill was worth quite a bit of money." She picked up her wineglass and leaned over Erika, refilling the glass from the bottle on that side of the bed. Erika nibbled playfully at Amber's breasts, running her hands down Amber's curves. Amber glanced at Brett. "I'm her broker."

These women didn't cease surprising Brett. "How long have you two been together?"

Amber, holding her glass, looked down into Erika's eyes. "We've known each other since college. We were roommates during junior and senior years. But tonight's the first time we've ever even kissed." She leaned down and kissed Erika, her naked body half-sprawled over Brett. When she came up for air, she looked at Brett. "I got tired of New York and Erika talked me into moving here, said she could line me up with some good clients, and I could crash with her until I decided where I wanted to live."

"When all the while you just wanted to live with her."

Erika looked at Brett with a mixture of surprise and realization.

Amber rolled over Brett and Erika to spoon herself against Erika's back, pulling her to her. "What do you think?"

"Amber?" Erika asked.

Amber ran her tongue along Erika's ear. "I've loved you for over five years now, but I've noticed how you always go for the butch ones, like Brett here."

"And you don't like her?"

Amber sat up a bit, leaned over Erika and ran a hand over Brett's bicep, then leaned forward to kiss her. "I said I love you. And I want to live with you, be with you, but I don't want to own you." She took Brett's hand and placed it between Erika's legs, moving it up and down to stroke her.

Erika moaned, moving Amber's hand down to join Brett's. Between gasps, as they slowly stroked her, she moaned, "I vote it's her bro, David. She was always giving him loans he didn't repay."

"You figure he was into drugs or gambling?" Amber asked, realizing they were playing another game.

"I dunno. She'd never tell me. Even when we were dating."

Erika began to writhe slightly. Brett gently led two of Amber's fingers up into her.

"Did you love her?" Brett asked, remembering the note.

"I cared for her deeply," Erika gasped. "But she said Lauren'd leave Rowan once she found out . . ." Amber looked up and met Brett's eyes, Brett pulled away, allowing Amber to pull Erika into her arms, to make her come while she was holding her. It was incredibly erotic, more than having a real-life porno flick, because she was starting to realize how much these women loved each other.

As soon as the two were asleep, Brett got up, washed, and dressed.

She went home.

During the short drive, she thought about the last things Erika had said—about how Jill seemed like a little lost child on so many levels and that she had apparently never heard anything about the little threesome Lauren, Rowan, and Jill had going on.

The fact that Lauren had repeatedly lied to her seemed to implicate her. But that didn't feel quite right. Plus, why would Lauren go off with Rowan only to kill Jill for her money? David seemed the more likely suspect, but then why would Lauren have lied for him?

Someone was lying about something. Or someone was lying about a number of things. Or maybe several people were lying about a helluva lot.

Then again, everybody could be lying about everything.

She pounded her head against the steering wheel. This investigation was going nowhere fast.

Two people stood to gain a great deal by Jill's death. Apparently, from Amber's remarks, Jill had even more money than Brett knew about. Now, thinking about the facts, just the facts, if she were to look at Rowan threatening Jill on the night Jill died, unless Rowan were responsible, that would be an incredible coincidence—and just a coincidence, and as Madeline always said, there was no such thing as coincidence.

So if, following Allie's thoughts and Madeline's sayings, Rowan was set up, that had to be part of the scheme as well. So someone set it up that Rowan and Jill would be at the bar at the same time, and that trouble would happen.

As soon as Brett realized she was actually listening to what Madeline said, she pounded her head on the steering wheel again.

Brett crawled into bed with Allie. Allie'd spent all day with Randi. But at least Randi now had a girlfriend. But still, when Brett rolled Allie onto her back and kissed her between her breasts, she couldn't help but wonder if what she was smelling was Allie, lotion, soap, or . . . Randi.

"Where were you?" Allie mumbled as Brett climbed on top of her.

"The campus. The bar. Jill's brother, David, who inherits half of her money, kept borrowing money from Jill, never repaying any of it. Quite probably for either gambling or drugs." She sucked on Allie's neck, laying her body on top of Allie's.

"Can you prove it?" Allie asked, arching up against Brett's thigh.

"I think her banker can, or her broker maybe—they'd know where her money was and where it was going," Brett pushed down against Allie, still kissing her neck, her ear, her earlobe. "If he owed people money, or needed more and more, that'd be a damned good motive. And he really was quite pissed when Jill inherited all those bucks, even though he says he wasn't." She worked her way down Allie's luscious body. "This is even more interesting when you realize he has a gun registered to him—a twenty-five caliber Beretta, which, as we both know is a rather small gun, and I see him as more of a three-fifty-seven sorta fellow, but that is the type of gun Rowan carries when she's off-duty." She loved and wanted Allie, even after her romp with Erika and Amber. Here was the thing: They were outside reality, they were the fantasy, and Allie was firmly embedded in the here and now.

Brett continued working down Allie's incredible body. "So maybe he didn't know too much about ballistics—that a gun to its bullet can be like a hand to its print. Either that or he was planning on briefly switching guns with Rowan. Since he had the same type of gun, she might not realize they'd been switched."

"He could've thought he could kill Jill with his gun, but blame Rowan. The one thing that doesn't fit is it seems like Jill had her own twenty-five Beretta on her that night at the bar. It was when Rowan knew Jill was packing that she pulled her own gun." Allie was squirming and arching and squirming some more.

Brett reached over for the lube and slicked her hands up. "But Dave might've given it to Jill as a gift, knowing that only if she were packing would Rowan pull her own gun—in front of so many witnesses. And Dave was pointing at Lauren and Rowan quite a bit that night at the bar." She flicked Allie's nipples with her tongue. She reached down to finger Allie, slowly sliding into her.

"Uh, oh, Brett . . ."

Brett slid into a rhythm.

"Oh, God, Brett . . ."

"Lesbian bed death my ass," Brett whispered into her ear, as she slid her fist into her. "I still want you. Do you want me?"

"Oh, fuck yes."

"Are you gonna come for me?" Brett felt her tightening around her fist.

"Yes. I . . . always . . . do . . ."

Brett felt Allie tightening around her fist, and she bit Allie's nipples when she started worrying her hand was about to break.

It was hard, it was painful. Brutal. And fuck yeah, it was hot.

"Brett . . . do you think you can pull together enough solid evidence to really prove what you said?" Allie finally said. After. A while after.

"Hold on, Allie, there's a few more pieces. Both Rowan and Lauren said they slept soundly through the night—"

"So Dave slipped a mickey into their drinks when they were at the bar."

Brett shook her head. "I dunno, Al. There's still a few missing pieces, but I don't know what to make of them. I'm not sure if folks have been lying to cover or out of embarrassment."

"What do you mean?"

"Listen to this. Lauren and Rowan got together when they were roommates during their sophomore year of college. Lauren was supposed to dump Jill that summer, between sophomore and junior years, but she didn't. Instead, she strung both women along and eventually they ended up as a threesome. The summer Lauren was supposed to dump Jill *but didn't* was the summer Jill inherited a small fortune from her gay uncle." Hopefully this would be enough to occupy Allie so she wouldn't ask too many questions about other things. Like how she found all this out.

"How'd you find all this out?" Allie was dumbfounded.

"Turning over a few of the right stones, snooping in the right places." Sleeping with the right women, she added silently, still luxuriating in it, even though she was quite aware of the potential fallout.

"They were a threesome."

"Yup. They were."

Allie paused, apparently digesting this bit of information. "Any sign of Rowan?"

"Well, I had a beer with her."

"What? A beer? But . . ."

"She didn't turn herself in. I just happened across her. Don't ask—just know I've been working my ass off on this mess for you."

"Brett . . ." Allie paused. "Where were you all night? Did you just get in?" She could tell Brett was trying to divert her attention and rush her, even though she did seem interested in what Brett had to report.

"Yeah, just walked in the door." This sucked, Brett thought, not being able to use her eyes on Allie—her puppy dog eyes—to not take her mind off the subject in other ways. "I had a couple of beers with Rowan, then stopped by a Denny's for a couple cups of coffee and some chow on my way home."

Chapter Twenty

Monday, 10:27 a.m.

The next morning, well, actually, just a few hours later, Brett got up, took a quick shower and went back upstairs to get dressed. She figured she'd get a head start on yet another action-packed day.

And yeah, she didn't really want Allie asking her too many more questions about yesterday. Last night. Where she got her information.

"God, please tell me this isn't Monday, and I don't have class," Allie said, coming up behind her and wrapping her arms around her.

Brett turned around. "You jump in the shower, I'll go down, put on the coffee and make us some breakfast."

"Oh, no time babe—busy day today. But I'll take you up on that coffee."

"It's a deal," Brett said, giving her a quick kiss and pat on the ass before she finished dressing and headed downstairs to put on the coffee. She figured Allie would at least go for some toast, so she set about making it. She suddenly thought maybe there really was a reason Maddy was quite handy. And then she saw someone dart from between their cars in the driveway.

Whoever it was ran to a Hummer and took off. A Hummer wasn't exactly big with the stealthy, but no one around their place owned a Hummer.

Brett walked out front and felt a set of eyes on her. She looked down the street. The cute little fagboy a few doors down was outside with his big yellow lab, washing his car. Now he was looking at her. She waved at him. He misfired his hose, spraying the dog instead.

"Oh, Astro, it's just a little water!" he yelled at the dog, who jumped when the spray hit him. Brett wondered if the fag was going to pull out his hair dryer again. One day she had seen him blow-drying his dog out in the driveway. It seemed rather peculiar behavior to her, but then again, he was a little fagboy, so what else should she expect?

And what had upset him so? She went through the motions of waving again, to try to figure out why he'd freaked and realized he'd seen her gun. Well for fuck's sake, you'd think he'd be used to it by now.

She walked around both vehicles, crawled under Allie's car, and walked back over to her Jimmy. That's when she noticed the envelope on the backseat. Fuck a duck, she thought, he'd broke into her goddamned car. At least it was a clean job—the locks weren't broken. She opened the back door.

She picked up the envelope and was about to go inside when she thought twice about it. Instead she sat and ripped open the package to find a stack of photos of her with Amber and Erika the night before—complete with negatives.

Blackmailers don't give up the negatives unless they had already made hundreds of copies of the incident in question.

Brett put everything neatly back into the envelope. The writing on it wasn't familiar, but it did look feminine.

She ran back inside. Allie was still in the shower. Thank God. Brett stuck her head into the bathroom. "Yo, hon, I've gotta run out and take care of a few things. I'm not sure when I'll be back."

"What? Brett?"

But Brett made sure she'd already taken off.

Outside of Erika and Amber's house she stopped and looked through the pictures again. Looking up at the house she could now see that the blinds weren't fully closed. Someone with a good camera could've stood at the front window and snapped these photos through them.

There were photos of Brett feeling up both Erika and Amber, of her fucking Amber with the strap-on when she was spread out on the coffee table, of the three of them naked together, going at it. The photos only stopped when they left the front room.

Brett went to the front of the house and looked in the dirt there and found what she was looking for—footprints. She put one of her feet next to one of them. These footprints were smaller than her own, but she had rather large feet for a woman. It left her with the thought that they were left by a woman.

Two women, actually. There were two different sets of prints, with slightly different sizes and tread marks on the soles.

Only one of her competitors employed women for this kind of work, and it was the same one she had been seeing way too much of lately.

She was at Jack's old office in twenty minutes. Her lockpicks did a quick job of the outside door. One fast, well-placed kick took out Jack's office door. Brett thought maybe she should've tried it first, see if it was even locked, but she was in too much of a mood.

"What?" Tina asked, standing behind the desk.

"Thanks for these," Brett threw the envelope on the desk. "Now, is there anything else you happened to see when you were following me around?"

"I . . . I don't know what you're talking about."

"Bullshit. You've been following me around, going to The House of Kinsey and talking with some of my friends, and this morning you dropped these pics off at my house. What would've happened if my girlfriend saw 'em?" She walked around the desk toward Tina, who backed away from her.

"Brett, I . . ." she tried to regain her composure, "I'm amazed you're up so early this morning." Her eyes flickered to a spot just over Brett's right shoulder.

Before Brett could do anything, everything went black.

"So this is the infamous Brett Higgins," Tina O'Rourke's friend Emma said, toeing the prone body on the floor. She'd just knocked Brett out with a bottle of booze. "She doesn't look so dangerous."

"I can't believe you did that! How the hell am I gonna get her to trust me now?"

"Oh, like she was gonna trust you before—especially after that photography session last night."

"I gave her the negatives."

"But who knows how many prints you made before that." Emma also knew about loopholes and finding the shit.

"Help me get her to the sofa," Tina said, picking Brett off the floor by her shoulders. Emma grabbed her feet and they gradually hefted Brett up and over to the sofa. Tina grabbed a handful of Kleenex and mopped Brett's brow, cleaning up the cheap Scotch from the bottle Emma had broken over her head. Emma cleaned up the glass and the rest of the Scotch that was on the floor behind Tina's desk.

Brett's features were etched clearly into her face. Each line was distinctly carved, beautifully handsome. In unconsciousness there was a certain peace to her. Tina wasn't sure if she could say it was the innocence of a child she now saw in Brett's face, but there was a simplicity she had never before seen.

She brushed the hair back off Brett's forehead. She had never before seen how much gray peppered her black hair, nor how lines were starting to form on Brett's face, even when in repose. The woman was just a hair beyond thirty, but somehow she looked both younger and older.

A sudden fantasy played through Tina's head. She imagined waking up next to Brett. She imagined Brett being the first thing she saw in the morning, and she Brett's. It was a simple fantasy, but hers nonetheless. She was surprised by it. She had never before had such a thought.

She wanted to feel Brett inside of her, she wanted to give herself to Brett. Wholly and totally. She looked up at Emma. "Leave us alone. Bring me back a bag of ice and then leave. Go out with Little Joey or something." Little Joey was one of the few of her father's employees that Tina thought was okay. Emma, her best friend, had been dating him on and off for several weeks now.

The world was black. Gentle hands were on her brow, brushing her hair back. Her Allie was back with her. Her and Allie, forever and ever. Eternity. Just like Allie's perfume. When they slow danced at the LesBiGay prom together, when Allie graduated from high school . . . The song was "I'll Always Love You." Whitney Houston. Quietly yearning. Wanting. Love to go on and on and on. And on. Like the fourth rose . . .

Her eyes struggled to open. Not Allie's blond hair. Not Allie's face, nor her smell. Not Allie. Some other woman. She closed her eyes.

There was a pain in her head. She remembered blacking out, something hitting her.

Her eyes shot open. Tina O'Rourke. Looking very concerned, mopping her brow with tissues . . .

"What the fuck's going on?" Brett sat bolt upright.

Tina jumped back, holding up her hands. "We're alone. Look around. I don't want to hurt you, I want to work *with* you."

Brett pulled out her gun and looked around the room. The manila envelope was right where she had left it on the desk. She checked the door, it was locked. They were alone.

"Brett, I don't want to hurt you," Tina was saying, slowly advancing on her.

"Then what's up with that shit?" Brett indicated the packet of photos with her gun. "Why're you following me around? Taking pictures? Trying to blackmail my ass?"

"I want to work *with* you. I want us to be *partners*."

"And you do this shit to me?"

"I wanted to find out something about you, figure out how best to get your interest. Your attention. And I wanted you to know that we were serious. We *are* capable. The only thing that's wrong is that these shit-head guys my father hired don't like taking orders from a woman. You know what that's like, don't you Brett?" She was getting cocky again. Actually, Brett preferred Tina cocky. She didn't think the helpless femme routine worked well with her.

Brett holstered her gun and went to inspect Jack's bar. "Where's the Scotch?"

"Emma broke it over your head."

Brett reached up to feel the lump on her skull, then turned to look in the trash. "Dewar's? Shit, you coulda at least used decent Scotch if you were gonna give me a headache like this." She glanced through the bar and decided on whiskey.

"You wanna cigar?" Tina asked.

"Hell, if Jack can't even drink single-malt Scotch, I'm scared shitless of the cigars he smokes." She picked up the envelope. "How many copies of these pics did you make?"

"None. What you've got is all of it." She went around the desk to Brett. "I don't need anymore midnight visits from you and Frankie. I don't want to work against you, Brett," she put her arm on Brett's neck, "I want to work with you."

"You mean for me?"

"With you. All I wanted to show you was that we're capable, we're good, and you're not infallible. I didn't mean coercion, or blackmail. I want to join forces. Emma and I decided to follow you last night when you were by my house. We took the pictures without thinking about it last night."

Brett sat back in Jack's chair, trying to imagine Jack giving the order to finish her off. Brett still, even years later, couldn't believe that Tina's father had once ordered her killed. "With me? Tina, lemme explain something to you, you're a nobody. What do I want with someone like you?"

"Your operation's fallen off since Frankie took over from you and Rick. It doesn't matter that you're back in the game. You see, I've got the size. You've got the experience. You scratch my back," she moved around the desk to stand, in her short skirt, directly in front of Brett. "And I do whatever you want."

Brett held up the envelope. "You already know I can have almost any woman I want." She stood up, towering over Tina. "As for size, well, under your leadership what's yours is gonna become mine. The only reason we're down from Rick's time is that we're only doing the legal stuff these days."

Tina took the envelope, pulling the photos out, one by one. "Everybody's got their weak spot, Brett."

Brett looked directly into Tina's eyes, not wanting her to know that she had hit the one chink in her armor, the one way she could possibly blackmail Brett Higgins. "Tina, photos won't get my compliance, dirty little threats or bottles broken over my head won't get my cooperation. I only work with people I trust, and right now there are only a few of 'em, and you ain't none of them."

Tina looked at her. "You know I won't ever forgive you for what you did to me."

"I notice you say what I did to you, not your father."

"This is personal."

"That's because you can't hold what I did to Jack against me, 'cause it's what you wanted—a chance." Brett downed her drink and headed for the door. She turned back to Tina as her hand was on the knob. "If you want your place here, you'll have to earn it. Claw your way to the top, like I did."

"If you walk out that door, I'm gonna be forced to take off the kid gloves with you, Brett."

Brett grabbed her, pinning her hands behind her back, her arms wrapped around her so that their bodies were pressed together, legs entwined, breasts against each other. "Don't even think of threatening me, Tina." Suddenly something came back to her. The other night at Jill's she knew she had been in that neighborhood before, and now she remembered when. That was also how Tina saw her—she spotted Brett when Brett went to check out Jill's house again. "Wednesday night, late Wednesday night, Thursday morning actually, did you notice anything strange happening at the house across the street from you?"

"What?"

Brett tightened her grasp on Tina's wrists. "The house across the street from you, Wednesday night, did you see anything?" If Tina was now involved in the life, then she'd be keeping hours as strange as Brett did and might've noticed something.

"You mean Jill's? I don't see how this has any importance—"

Brett could feel her breath on her face, they were so close. "Yeah. Jill St. Claire's."

Tina looked all around, not meeting her gaze, so Brett tightened her grip further still so that their bodies were almost melded together. "I dunno. I got home real late, heard some yelling, and two women left. Or more like they were chased out by that bitch."

"You saw her after they left?"

"Yes," she whispered. "She was out on the porch and her brother and his girlfriend were there, too."

Brett whipped her around, pressing her into the door with the full length of her body. "Did you notice anything else?"

"Why, was she some kinky playmate of yours?"

"You want kink?" Brett pushed her thigh into Tina's crotch. "I'll give you so much kink your lil' straight-laced panties will think they're a sponge. Now tell me, did you notice anything else?"

Tina's legs opened a bit more against Brett's pressure. "I . . . I thought it was funny her brother parked down the street."

Brett began grinding her thigh against Tina. "He parked down the street?"

"Yes. I don't know if Jill's friends knew he was even there." She was breathing heavier now, moving her body against Brett's.

"Did you hear or see anything else that night?"

Tina's nipples strained up. "No . . . no, I didn't. I had to . . . had to get up early the next morning, and I was dead tired . . ."

"I've seen how you look at me—how you watch me with other women."

"I don't know . . . what you mean," Tina moaned.

"Did you enjoy watching me last night? Watching me doing those women? Did you wish you were them, huh Tina?"

Tina's eyes shot open and she looked at Brett, arching against her.

"Brett . . ." was all she could manage a moment later when Brett pulled away and left.

Brett climbed into the Jimmy and noticed the scrap of paper on the floor. She picked it up to throw it away, but glanced at it first. Yup, a shopping list. In a feminine hand, it was a shopping list with the usual items—eggs, butter, bread, milk . . .

But the handwriting was familiar. She tried to remember from where, and where she had picked up the list. She sat in her car trying to remember . . . outside of Diane and David's. Allie had pointed it out on Brett's shoe. She had assumed it was a list Diane had written for David. But where was the feminine script familiar from?

Chapter Twenty-one

Monday, 5:27 p.m.

Brett pulled up into Lauren and Rowan's driveway. She knew Lauren was lying, and she had to find out why.

It took Lauren a few minutes to answer the door. She was dressed in a neat, double-breasted pinstripe suit in a deep olive. Her black hose and pumps highlighted her legs, making them even more shapely.

"Ummm, somebody's here, lemme call you back," Lauren said into the cordless phone in her hand. She listened for a moment, said her good-byes then hung up. "Sorry about that," she said, leading Brett into the living room and sitting on the sofa.

Brett glanced back at the phone, a sleek black module with a little display screen on the back of the handset. "It's okay, I just had a few more questions about you, Rowan, and Jill."

"Oh, I thought we covered all that the other day." She took off her shoes and rubbed her feet gratefully. "God, I hate those things."

"Why did you lie to me?"

Lauren looked up sharply. "What?"

"You lied to me. About when you and Rowan got together, and about when you and Jill broke up. Why?"

Lauren looked away. "I guess I was hoping to . . . to make it look less like Rowan stole me from Jill. That way it would seem less like they had a real reason to hate each other enough to . . . to commit murder."

"So you're saying you think Rowan did it?"

"No! Not at all! You don't know Rowan like I do! She could never do such a thing!"

"Then why do you feel the need to cover up for her? And don't you understand how easily lies like these are uncovered?"

"You're the only one who asked the questions, though. All the cops needed to know was that Jill was my ex, and had been accosting me whenever the three of us ran into each other." She faced Brett, tears running down her face. "I know you're only trying to help, but it seemed like as good a time as any to start covering. After all, it's not like I can even supply Rowan with a good alibi."

Brett looked around the room. Everything was still tidy and clean. "What were you doing with Jill and Rowan the summer between your sophomore and junior years?"

"What do you mean?" She looked stunned.

"More lies, Lauren, how 'bout telling me the truth for a change? You were with Rowan and were supposed to go home and dump Jill, but you didn't, you didn't dump her because she had inherited a helluva lot of money, and that was tough to leave, wasn't it?"

"I couldn't dump her because once I saw her again, I realized I still loved her. Must be tough for somebody like you to understand, but I loved her." She turned to face Brett. "Have you ever loved two women at the same time?"

Brett could suddenly understand. She had loved two women

simultaneously, but she had chosen the more traditional route of breaking up the triangle—she dumped Storm for Allie.

"I thought if they got to know each other better, maybe something would happen, or at least I would find out which one was right for me." She looked at Brett. "It didn't happen the way I had planned. I'm embarrassed by it all."

"I already know you became a threesome."

Lauren shook her head. "How do you know all this?" She got up and began tidying the already neat room. "It's like you've been following me for years or something."

"Rowan told me."

Lauren's eyes lit up. She fell to her knees in front of Brett, taking both her hands. Her eyes bright, she said, "You've seen Rowan?"

"Yes. So what happened?"

"No, where did you see Rowan? Where is she? How is she?" Tears were again streaming down her face.

"I ran into her. She's doing the best she can, being on the lam. Now what really happened?"

"Petty jealousy. Every way we turned, somebody was always feeling left out of something. And Jill wasn't too happy that Rowan and I spent so much more time together. She said she could support us all, so why didn't we just drop out of school and all move in together right then?" The tears had stopped, and she wiped what was left with the handful of tissues she had in her hand. "But Rowan really wanted to be a cop. She felt like she had some sort of a mission. Finally, we had to choose—and I mean all of us. I think all of us were in love with each other, but it just couldn't work." She looked at Brett. "I think Jill had her heart broken two ways, because she was also in love with Rowan. But that love turned to anger when she became the one left in the cold. She couldn't understand what happened."

Brett thought that if Lauren was putting on an act, it was a damned good one, and the girl should be onstage. "Is there anything else? Anything at all? Don't lie to me again."

"No. Just if you see Rowan again, tell her I love and miss her."

"Tell me this, Lauren, wasn't it tough walking away from so much money?"

"I loved Jill, but she had so many problems. Forceful, an awful temper, sometimes violent, and she wasn't willing to do anything about it. Yes, it was tough, but I know I made the right decision. I took Rowan to Jill's that night because I still wanted Jill in my life, and she really wasn't happy, and I knew that maybe if she could finish with the past, she could find herself a happier future. I guess that won't be happening now."

"Did you happen to see anyone outside when you left Jill's? Or maybe a suspicious car or something?"

Lauren shook her head sorrowfully. "No. I can't remember shit. There were some cars in the street, some in driveways. I just remember Rowan pointing out a beat-up truck, saying something about it shouldn't even be allowed on the streets."

Brett went to the front window, taking in the street outside. "Y'know, I'm kinda thirsty. Ya got any beer?"

Lauren looked vaguely surprised by the request, but slowly nodded. "Yes, yes I think so." She went to the kitchen to get one.

Brett went over to the phone punched in *67 and hit the redial button, grinning that her guess was right—the display on the back of the phone showed the number as it was dialed. She hung up before it could even ring, quickly hitting *69 to find out the last number to call the house. This was a number she knew.

When Lauren returned with the beer, Brett said she'd forgotten an important appointment and left.

Brett pulled into her driveway and sat in the Jimmy, staring at the house.

"What are you doing, casing the joint?" Allie asked, coming up to her.

Brett pulled out of her reverie to look at Allie. "Thinking. Something's not adding up. Or else two and two are adding up to three or five."

"We are talking about the current sitch, right?"

"Yeah." Brett climbed out of the car, going with Allie back into the house. "Does this writing look familiar to you?" she asked, holding out the grocery list.

Allie studied it for a moment, then walked to the kitchen table and picked up the photocopy of the note she'd brought home the day before from the bookstore. She held the two side-by-side. "Yup, it sure does." She showed Brett that the writing matched.

Brett threw herself down onto the couch, propping her feet on the coffee table. She grabbed the cordless phone off the end table. Pulling a piece of paper from her pocket, she quickly dialed. Stephen picked up on the first ring.

Brett cut to the chase. "Is Rowan there?"

"Who is this?"

"Brett Higgins. Stephen—we met the other night."

"Oh, yeah, right. No, I'm sorry, she left a little bit ago."

"She left? What'd she have, a hot date or something?" Allie sat down next to Brett, paying close attention to everything she could hear.

"No. Don't I wish. Somebody around here needs to get laid. That bitch Lauren called and talked her into heading back down there."

"Heading down here? She's wanted for murder!" It was Stephen's number that showed up as the last one called on Lauren's phone when Brett had checked. Lauren had been talking with Rowan on the phone when Brett arrived.

"Yeah, well, she was going through withdrawals and called Lauren who told her how bad it all looked, her running away and all, and convinced her to at least come down so they could talk about it in person."

"Okay, Stevie, thanks for the info. I'll catch ya around." She hung up, then sat back in the couch, still holding the phone. She turned to face Allie. "Money, love, and revenge are all intermixed. Dave and Lauren will inherit. Lauren dumped Jill for Rowan, but Rowan also dumped Jill for Lauren. They were a threesome. Lauren intimated that Jill had physically abused her at times."

"Um, but that sounds more like reasons for Jill to want revenge on Lauren and Rowan, but only a bit of a reason for Lauren or Rowan to want revenge. Money, on the other hand, can be quite a motivating force."

Brett pulled Erika's phone number from her pocket. But she couldn't talk to her in front of Allie. "Lauren lied to me. I went there this morning, after Tina's, and she played that she didn't know where Rowan was. But Lauren was talking with Rowan when I got there."

"Hold on. Tina?"

"Get this—I remembered something about Jill's neighborhood. I remembered this morning that Tina lived there, so I went to see if she knew anything."

"Why didn't you tell me?"

"We don't seem to interrogate well together. If Lauren's got Rowan coming back down here, something's going on—I just wish I knew what it was. Why don't you check with Randi, see if there's been any new developments she's heard of. I'll check with Artie, see if he knows anything new."

Allie picked up the cordless. "Sounds like a plan."

"I'm gonna check my e-mail while I'm at it," Brett said, pulling out her cellular and going into the study. She made sure to close the door behind her. Last night, Amber had cut off Erika when she was about to say something. Something was scratching at the back of Brett's mind, and it just wasn't right. She had to know what Erika had almost said, and needed to figure out what was going on.

Erika answered on the third ring. "Hello?"

"Heya," Brett found herself remembering the night before, remembering silky, toned thighs, warm flesh, and the taste of both women on her lips.

"Why Brett Higgins, are you calling to find out if you can come over again tonight?"

Brett sighed audibly. "No, I think I have to work. But you know I'd love to nuzzle into you again. Love to taste you, and feel you . . ."

Brett heard another phone being picked up on Erika's side. "I want in if this is turning into phone sex," Amber said. Erika giggled.

"I prefer up close and personal," Brett said. "I was just calling to find out what Jill said to Erika."

"What?"

"When you two broke it off. Last night you said something about Jill being sure Lauren would dump Rowan—"

"When she found out Rowan was screwing around with some chick named Diane."

Brett still couldn't believe what she'd heard when Allie came into the study. "Allie, a lot of people've tried a lot of different things to get away with murder, but has anyone ever tried looking like the most obvious suspect?"

"Everything's been tried and done. *Especially* that."

"Rowan and Diane were having an affair."

"You have so got to be shitting me."

"Okay, so if Lauren's a bad guy," Brett said, "and she's got Rowan coming back down, then something bad's about to happen, and I'd reckon it'll happen at their home sweet home."

"So you think we should head down there and keep an eye on the place?"

"Can't hurt. Do you think you could get Randi to keep an eye on Dave and Diane's? I'm not convinced they're innocent, either."

Chapter Twenty-two

Monday, 8:37 p.m.

Brett and Allie decided to drive separately in case one of them had to tail anyone. Brett didn't like that this stakeout was so impromptu. For one thing, she didn't have any Ding Dongs, and she could really go for one right about now.

She wondered if she could swing by a store and lay in some supplies. Allie was heading to the same place she was, and she'd kick Brett's butt if Brett showed up late with bags of treats. At least she had her soda. She parked not too far down the street from Allie on the near side of the house. She stayed under cover as she ran to Allie's car and climbed in.

"That's Dave's truck, isn't it?" Brett said, indicating the battered pick-up sitting in Rowan and Lauren's driveway.

"It sure is. No reason he should be here—unless he's involved. Or out for some vengeance. A real lose-lose situation."

Allie's cell rang. "Hello? Well, I know where Dave is—we're at Rowan and Lauren's and he's here . . . No, I'm not sure if Diane's here, we just got here ourselves . . . Yes, Brett's with me . . . I'll let you know." She hung up the phone. "That was Randi, calling to let me know no one's at Dave and Diane's."

"Yeah, I figured as much. Tell ya what, let me case the joint. I'll let you know what's the what, 'kay?"

"Yeah. Ringers off, guns chambered."

"Right on." Brett checked to make sure her .357 was chambered so it carried an extra bullet and was ready to go, then made sure her cell was in her pocket and on vibrate. She leaned over and kissed Allie quickly and slid out of the car.

Not knowing what to expect, she cautiously approached the house, figuring there were maybe four people inside—Rowan, Lauren, Dave, and Diane.

She scurried across the lawn, trying to remember the layout of the house from her prior visits. When she walked by Dave's truck she laid a careful hand on the hood—it was still warm. He hadn't been there long.

The only way Rowan and Diane could get to the money was via their respective partners, so things did not look good for Lauren and Dave. That is, if it was Rowan and Diane. Something still wasn't fitting though. Brett wasn't sure if Dave and Lauren would inherit if they had offed Jill, for one thing. And if they didn't actually inherit, neither would Rowan nor Diane if they in turn killed Lauren and Dave.

Brett glanced up and wondered if she could enter the house unsuspected through the upstairs. She could possibly work her way up to grab onto part of the roof if she were to jump from the fence. Her next choice was the omnipresent back door all these older homes had.

Brett considered Artie's involvement. He had given Brett a good deal of important information. And had also been the one who arranged for Rowan's escape from jail. Maybe that was how he figured into it—to ensure enough loose ends were left there would be no way Rowan could be convicted. Maybe he was Rowan's safety net. He had seen Brett as an outside source that could be led into the entire maze and find out all the information and loopholes that he, Rowan, and Diane needed someone on the outside to discover and testify about.

Brett circled the house, trying to figure out where everyone was. Peeking in through the various blinds and drapes as much as she could with them being largely closed, she couldn't see anyone, so decided to try the back door.

It was locked.

The Artie angle made all of this seem well setup. Jill was murdered for a reason. Lauren and Dave would inherit, and Dave needed money bad. He would be the logical suspect if Rowan were cleared. And Brett was seemingly close to clearing Rowan. She knew you couldn't inherit from a person you'd killed. If Rowan and Diane killed Dave and Lauren, making it seem as if Dave and Lauren had killed Jill, they'd end up with nothing. The money that would've gone to Dave and Lauren would go somewhere else.

As would Dave's share if he killed Jill. And Brett was willing to bet that money would end up with Lauren. Jill was bound to have a good lawyer to set up her will, so it would contain specifics on lots of different contingencies—such as if either Lauren or Dave died before Jill.

Brett stuffed her gun in the front of her pants, listening closely at the back door. She pulled out her picks, quickly playing them into the lock until she pushed the bolt back and quietly opened the door.

She had four players, possibly five, if Artie was involved. So that allowed for many different combinations, if it were indeed two people involved. Of course, it could be just one, or maybe three . . . or four . . . or, hell, so long as she was getting stupid about it, maybe *everybody* was involved! Ha! That was it—they were *all* guilty!

But if Lauren and Rowan missed the threesome thing, then why hadn't they just hooked up again with Jill directly? Why would Lauren choose Rowan over Jill if she really wanted the money? Because she couldn't stand Jill, and needed someone to show how easy it would be to get the money from Jill? And what the hell was up with Diane and Rowan having an affair? Was it truth or just Jill's hopeful fiction?

"I shtill don' unnerstand whash going on." It was Rowan's voice. Her quite drunken voice.

Almost soundlessly, Brett crept across the kitchen until she could see out into the living room. Rowan stood, or rather leaned, against the fireplace that faced the sofa. Lauren sat on the sofa and Dave stood near the bar, holding a bottle of Absolut vodka. Diane leaned rather haggardly against the arm of the sofa.

Brett suddenly knew that the thoughts skirting her mind for some time were right on the mark.

"Dave and I realized we're the ones who are going to inherit that pile of money from Jill," Lauren said from the couch. "So we should, most logically, be the chief suspects."

Brett noticed Dave fiddling with the vodka bottle when his back was to the rest of the room. Rowan was having enough troubles standing up to notice much else.

"Are you shaying you killed her?" Rowan slurred.

"They . . . they . . ." Diane tried to say, but she couldn't quite get her act together enough to say it.

Dave walked up to Rowan, taking the glass in one hand, filling it up from the vodka bottle, and giving it back to her. He then reached for it back. "Or maybe you've had enough—"

Rowan pulled the glass from his reach and took a long swallow. "Don't be shilly, I'm fine. Jus' fine. See?" She extended one arm and raised it so the tip of her index finger not only missed her nose, but her entire head as well.

Dave was deliberately getting her drunk—and spiking her drinks with something. Probably something that'd kill her. Brett glanced back at the bar and saw a bottle of rubbing alcohol, isopropanol, peeking out from behind the other bottles.

Brett couldn't remember all the details of isopropanol, but knew that it would pack a helluva wallop, causing a lot of trouble that would be hard to diagnose at the hospital. She was willing to guess that Dave and Lauren were doing the isopropanol trick on both Rowan and Diane, while they were likely drinking water.

Rowan tossed the rest of the glass back with a quick gesture and then slowly slid to the floor. She was out in seconds.

Brett figured she didn't have long if Rowan and Diane were gonna make it. She wished she could risk calling 911, or even Allie, but of course, she couldn't.

Lauren casually stood and walked to Rowan's prone body. She put her fingers on her neck, then her wrist, watching her wristwatch while she did so. She then walked to the desk and pulled a piece of paper out of it.

Brett suddenly realized Dave was nowhere to be seen. She cautiously turned around, wondering where he could have disappeared to. As she inched toward the other end of the kitchen her foot hit something and she heard the loud snap of the mousetrap she had set off.

"What was that?" It was Diane's weary voice from the other room. Brett kicked the trap off the toe of her boot and looked up—right at Dave, who smacked Brett's gun out of her hands as soon as she looked up from the mousetrap.

"Just the rat trap going off in here," Dave said, staring right into Brett's eyes and aiming a .45 directly at her. "I wouldn't even think about it," he continued when Brett glanced at her gun. "Turn around and spread 'em." He frisked Brett, uncovered her switchblade, and tossed it to the side. "You're just covered with illegal shit, ain't ya? Writer my ass."

"Oh, fuck!" Lauren cried as she entered the kitchen. "What're we gonna do with her?" she asked Dave.

"Don't worry, I've got ideas for everything."

"What do you mean by that?"

"I did some research, especially once she and her little girlyfriend got involved in it all. When she showed up to talk to Diane and me right after stopping by your place, I figured I'd better be prepared. What it all comes down to is that it seems we're standing here with a regular celebrity. You see, Lauren, she wasn't pulling your leg about having recently retired from a life of crime—she was so far in, she faked her own death to get out of it. So I'm thinking we should blow her brains out and dump her body in the river, which would make it look like one of her competitors got a hold of her. That or we just blow her brains out here and leave her here."

"That wouldn't be too smart, now would it Dave?" Brett asked. "You'd get blood all over everything." It all finally clicked right into place. She understood it all completely now.

"But it would be pretty damned easily explainable—since your little Lazarus routine, it seems that you've taken to blowing out the brains of various bad guys. So you came in here, to save Lauren from Rowan, but I was also here. You blew off Rowan's head, and all I knew was that there was an armed woman in the house shooting—so I found one of Rowan's guns and shot you by accident."

"Actually, I meant that your little girlfriend over here is such a clean freak, if you got blood all over, she'd spend the rest of your lives together cleaning it up—because I don't think blood would quite fit the decor of the rest of the room."

"Smart ass," Dave said, shoving Brett's back as they led her back into the living room.

"So you two are seeing each other," Brett said, following his direction.

"Go fuck yourself," Lauren said, raising Brett's own gun at her. How humiliating, Brett thought.

"Ooo," Brett exclaimed, studying Lauren quickly before she sat, "you should know I love a girl with a gun." Lauren apparently didn't find this amusing, raising the gun as if to hit Brett with it.

Dave stayed her hand. "No. Let's decide what we're going to do before we start mutilating the body."

The summer breeze blew the front drapes open just enough so Brett caught a flash of blond hair. She needed to buy a bit of time. Everything would be all right if she could just buy some time. "Oh, c'mon," she said, "as long as we're playing out this entire ending, you've got to tell me the how and why of it all—after all, I need some sort of a confession to use against you once I escape from your dastardly plot."

Lauren smirked. "We don't have time."

Two guns on her. If the two would just get close enough, she might have a chance to get the guns before getting shot, but since they were several feet apart, it wasn't an option. But they couldn't both keep covering her—after all, what would be the point? "Is it that you two just started up with the idea of putting the blame on the homophobes?"

"Yeah, that's what happened," Dave said. "Then, as we started to get into it, laying all the plans, we realized this was a much better idea."

"If Rowan hadn't taken off, we would've just let her take the blame," Lauren said, "but we did have to involve Diane once things got rolling. After all, put her on the stand and she would admit she couldn't remember leaving Jill's."

"So Dave did the actual deed. And although Jill was alive when Lauren and Rowan left, she wasn't when you two left."

"And I suppose you'll also leave a few traces that Diane and Rowan were having an affair."

"Of course," Lauren said. "That did it, once Dave and I figured that one out, if we had any second thoughts, they were gone." Her face was deadly serious. Diane and Rowan really were having an affair.

"And now, Rowan realizes she ain't gonna get out of it, so she brings Diane over here to do her in when she kills herself."

Just then, the doorbell rang. Again, the three looked at each other. The doorbell became more persistent. "Ignore it," Dave told Lauren, who was glancing toward the door. "Nobody else should be coming."

Just then the doorbell was replaced with a knocking. "Hey—c'mon, open up! I know you're in there!" Brett recognized the voice—but Allie had pitched it weird, low and gravelly, so, since Dave and Lauren didn't know her too well, they didn't recognize it. "Your fuckin' piece a shit truck is in the middle of the goddamned street blocking traffic!"

"Damn," Lauren said. "Cover her." Dave nodded and moved so he was no longer in view of the door. Lauren crossed to the door, opening it so her gun was hidden from the caller by the door. "Yes?"

All Brett saw was the black of her briefcase. Allie swung the case at Lauren, sending her and her gun flying. Brett dropped to the floor and did a quick leg sweep, sending Dave tumbling to the ground. She threw herself on his back, pinning him with her knees while she pounded his arm on the ground until he let go of the gun. It went skittering across the room.

She quickly checked to make sure Allie was all right, then dove after the gun, grabbing it to cover Dave.

Allie backed up next to her, covering Lauren. She'd gotten Lauren's gun about as quickly as Brett'd gotten Dave's.

Randi came charging in with her gun drawn. "What's going on here?"

Epilogue

Friday, 11:57 p.m.

"You not only have nine lives, but the luck of the devil as well," Rowan yelled over the music to Brett, who sat on the far side of the table. Allie was off chatting with Ski and Randi. This was the first time they had come to the Rainbow Room since the night Jill had been killed. "You keep barely missing having your ass shot off, and then you keep getting away with it."

As it turned out, that fateful Wednesday was not the first time Rowan, Lauren, Dave, Diane, and Jill had come into contact with each other all at once. During college, Rowan and Lauren had of course met Dave—after all, they were so close to Jill it only made sense that they'd meet her family.

But a few years ago, Rowan and Lauren were at the bar when Jill showed up with Dave and Diane, introducing Diane fully into the mix. Rowan and she had initially bonded over the incredible mess and then the relationship blossomed. Meanwhile, Lauren and Dave hooked up as well. Everyone was playing everyone else.

"I'm still waiting to hear what a Toblerone is," Kurt yelled at Brett.

"Oh. A Toblerone is a candy bar that comes in, well, like pieces," Brett said. "Most commonly twelve pieces. A Toblerone in the sense I meant it was . . . er, well . . . a dozen orgasms in one session."

"Hot fuck!" Frankie said. "You dames are lucky!"

Brett looked around at all her friends gathered in this sort of celebration: Madeline and Leisa, Randi and Ski, Frankie and Kurt, Allie and Rowan . . . Brett wondered if she should worry about that.

But she couldn't help but think how lucky she really was. On Monday night, Allie had waited for Brett for a while, then went to check out the place herself, getting nervous about why Brett hadn't contacted her yet. She saw what was happening through the front window, and called Randi, who was already on her way over.

Because of this, and immediate identification of the symptoms and poisons used, there were no fatalities. Dave and Lauren had fed Rowan and Diane cocktails of vodka, isopropyl alcohol, Benadryl, and tranquilizers. The Benadryl was to keep them from throwing up before the isopropyl could work its deadly trick. Isopropyl is the fastest acting of the alcohol family, and Dave and Lauren had decided that if anything went wrong, it could be explained as an accident—after all, the form of it they had used was rubbing alcohol, which is commonly found around the house, but Brett couldn't quite figure out how someone could mistakenly drink that much of it.

Dave had talked Diane into taking Jill into the Rainbow Room the night of Jill's murder. She ended up taking Jill aside and recommending the bar as a way to help get her brother Dave into a better mental state in his acceptance of Jill's sexuality. Lauren talked Rowan into it, and then into stopping by Jill's. They had every step of it laid out.

The song ended and a warped one came on, sounding a bit like a house mix. Allie waved goodbye to Randi and Ski and headed back toward the table just as Brett felt two sets of hands on her. One set guided her face up and around, till her lips met with a different soft, sweet pair. She pulled away just as a tongue began to press its way into her mouth.

"Long time no see, stud," Amber said. "You gonna come home with us and play tonight?"

Brett looked around to see that Erika stood on her other side, touching her in a more than friendly manner. Rowan and Allie stood, watching in open-mouthed fascination.

Erika nodded to them. "This woman fucks like there's no tomorrow."

THE NEXT WORLD by Ursula Steck. 240 pp. Anna's friend Mido is threatened and eventually disappears . . . 1-59493-024-4 $12.95

CALL SHOTGUN by Jaime Clevenger. 240 pp. Kelly gets pulled back into the world of private investigation . . . 1-59493-016-3 $12.95

52 PICKUP by Bonnie J. Morris and E.B. Casey. 240 pp. 52 hot, romantic tales—one for every Saturday night of the year. 1-59493-026-0 $12.95

GOLD FEVER by Lyn Denison. 240 pp. Kate's first love, Ashley, returns to their home town, where Kate now lives . . . 1-1-59493-039-2 $12.95

RISKY INVESTMENT by Beth Moore. 240 pp. Lynn's best friend and roommate needs her to pretend Chris is his fiancé. But nothing is ever easy. 1-59493-019-8 $12.95

HUNTER'S WAY by Gerri Hill. 240 pp. Homicide detective Tori Hunter is forced to team up with the hot-tempered Samantha Kennedy. 1-59493-018-X $12.95

CAR POOL by Karin Kallmaker. 240 pp. Soft shoulders, merging traffic and slippery when wet . . . Anthea and Shay find love in the car pool. 1-59493-013-9 $12.95

NO SISTER OF MINE by Jeanne G'Fellers. 240 pp. Telepathic women fight to coexist with a patriarchal society that wishes their eradication. ISBN 1-59493-017-1 $12.95

ON THE WINGS OF LOVE by Megan Carter. 240 pp. Stacie's reporting career is on the rocks. She has to interview bestselling author Cheryl, or else! ISBN 1-59493-027-9 $12.95

WICKED GOOD TIME by Diana Tremain Braund. 224 pp. Does Christina need Miki as a protector . . . or want her as a lover? ISBN 1-59493-031-7 $12.95

THOSE WHO WAIT by Peggy J. Herring. 240 pp. Two brilliant sisters—in love with the same woman! ISBN 1-59493-032-5 $12.95

ABBY'S PASSION by Jackie Calhoun. 240 pp. Abby's bipolar sister helps turn her world upside down, so she must decide what's most important. ISBN 1-59493-014-7 $12.95

PICTURE PERFECT by Jane Vollbrecht. 240 pp. Kate is reintroduced to Casey, the daughter of an old friend. Can they withstand Kate's career? ISBN 1-59493-015-5 $12.95

PAPERBACK ROMANCE by Karin Kallmaker. 240 pp. Carolyn falls for tall, dark and . . . female . . . in this classic lesbian romance. ISBN 1-59493-033-3 $12.95

DAWN OF CHANGE by Gerri Hill. 240 pp. Susan ran away to find peace in remote Kings Canyon—then she met Shawn . . . ISBN 1-59493-011-2 $12.95

DOWN THE RABBIT HOLE by Lynne Jamneck. 240 pp. Is a killer holding a grudge against FBI Agent Samantha Skellar? ISBN 1-59493-012-0 $12.95

SEASONS OF THE HEART by Jackie Calhoun. 240 pp. Overwhelmed, Sara saw only one way out—leaving . . . ISBN 1-59493-030-9 $12.95

TURNING THE TABLES by Jessica Thomas. 240 pp. The 2nd Alex Peres Mystery. *From ghosties and ghoulies and long leggity beasties . . .* ISBN 1-59493-009-0 $12.95

FOR EVERY SEASON by Frankie Jones. 240 pp. Andi, who is investigating a 65-year-old murder, meets Janice, a charming district attorney . . . ISBN 1-59493-010-4 $12.95

LOVE ON THE LINE by Laura DeHart Young. 240 pp. Kay leaves a younger woman behind to go on a mission to Alaska . . . will she regret it? ISBN 1-59493-008-2 $12.95

UNDER THE SOUTHERN CROSS by Claire McNab. 200 pp. Lee, an American travel agent, goes down under and meets Australian Alex, and the sparks fly under the Southern Cross. ISBN 1-59493-029-5 $12.95

SUGAR by Karin Kallmaker. 240 pp. Three women want sugar from Sugar, who can't make up her mind. ISBN 1-59493-001-5 $12.95

FALL GUY by Claire McNab. 200 pp. 16th Detective Inspector Carol Ashton Mystery. ISBN 1-59493-000-7 $12.95

ONE SUMMER NIGHT by Gerri Hill. 232 pp. Johanna swore to never fall in love again—but then she met the charming Kelly . . . ISBN 1-59493-007-4 $12.95

TALK OF THE TOWN TOO by Saxon Bennett. 181 pp. Second in the series about wild and fun loving friends. ISBN 1-931513-77-5 $12.95

LOVE SPEAKS HER NAME by Laura DeHart Young. 170 pp. Love and friendship, desire and intrigue, spark this exciting sequel to *Forever and the Night.* ISBN 1-59493-002-3 $12.95

TO HAVE AND TO HOLD by Peggy J. Herring. 184 pp. By finally letting down her defenses, will Dorian be opening herself to a devastating betrayal? ISBN 1-59493-005-8 $12.95

WILD THINGS by Karin Kallmaker. 228 pp. Dutiful daughter Faith has met the perfect man. There's just one problem: she's in love with his sister. ISBN 1-931513-64-3 $12.95

SHARED WINDS by Kenna White. 216 pp. Can Emma rebuild more than just Lanny's marina? ISBN 1-59493-006-6 $12.95

THE UNKNOWN MILE by Jaime Clevenger. 253 pp. Kelly's world is getting more and more complicated every moment. ISBN 1-931513-57-0 $12.95

TREASURED PAST by Linda Hill. 189 pp. A shared passion for antiques leads to love. ISBN 1-59493-003-1 $12.95

SIERRA CITY by Gerri Hill. 284 pp. Chris and Jesse cannot deny their growing attraction . . . ISBN 1-931513-98-8 $12.95

ALL THE WRONG PLACES by Karin Kallmaker. 174 pp. Sex and the single girl—Brandy is looking for love and usually she finds it. Karin Kallmaker's first *After Dark* erotic novel. ISBN 1-931513-76-7 $12.95

WHEN THE CORPSE LIES A Motor City Thriller by Therese Szymanski. 328 pp. Butch bad-girl Brett Higgins is used to waking up next to beautiful women she hardly knows. Problem is, this one's dead. ISBN 1-931513-74-0 $12.95

GUARDED HEARTS by Hannah Rickard. 240 pp. Someone's reminding Alyssa about her secret past, and then she becomes the suspect in a series of burglaries. ISBN 1-931513-99-6 $12.95

ONCE MORE WITH FEELING by Peggy J. Herring. 184 pp. Lighthearted, loving, romantic adventure. ISBN 1-931513-60-0 $12.95

TANGLED AND DARK A Brenda Strange Mystery by Patty G. Henderson. 240 pp. When investigating a local death, Brenda finds two possible killers—one diagnosed with Multiple Personality Disorder. ISBN 1-931513-75-9 $12.95

WHITE LACE AND PROMISES by Peggy J. Herring. 240 pp. Maxine and Betina realize sex may not be the most important thing in their lives. ISBN 1-931513-73-2 $12.95

UNFORGETTABLE by Karin Kallmaker. 288 pp. Can Rett find love with the cheerleader who broke her heart so many years ago? ISBN 1-931513-63-5 $12.95